"I, Elizabeth, take thee, Robert,
to my lawful wedded husband,
for richer, for poorer. . ."

As the beautiful words of the wedding service reached her, Coralie became conscious of an odd little ache in her breast; a tightening deep inside her in the region of her heart.

Now, watching as Rob bent his dark head closer to Liz's shining coppery curls, Coralie admitted just for one brief moment that she felt envious of Liz standing at the altar with the man she loved, while she, Coralie, was merely striving for friendship with the man who held her heart in the hollow of his hand. . .

Bantam Circle of Love Romances
Ask your bookseller for the books you have missed

Dear Friend,

Enter the Circle of Love—and travel to faraway places with romantic heroes. . .

We read hundreds of novels and, each month select the very best—from the finest writers around the world—to bring you these wonderful love stories . . . stories that let *you* share in a variety of beautiful romantic experiences.

With Circle of Love Romances, you treat yourself to a romantic holiday—anytime, anywhere. And because we want to please you, won't you write and let us know your comments and suggestions?

Meanwhile, welcome to the Circle of Love— we don't think you'll ever want to leave!

Best,

Cathy Camhy
Editor

CIRCLE OF LOVE™

Thread of Scarlet

Rachel Murray

BANTAM BOOKS
TORONTO · NEW YORK · LONDON · SYDNEY

THREAD OF SCARLET

*A Bantam Book/published by arrangement with
Robert Hale, Ltd.*

PRINTING HISTORY

*This edition first published in Great Britain 1980
CIRCLE OF LOVE, the garland and the ring designs are
trademarks of Bantam Books, Inc.*

Bantam edition/May 1982

ISBN 0-553-21512-4

Published simultaneously in the United States and Canada

---

*Bantam Books are published by Bantam Books, Inc. Its
trademark, consisting of the words "Bantam Books" and the
portrayal of a rooster, is Registered in U.S. Patent and
Trademark Office and in other countries. Marca Registrada.
Bantam Books, Inc., 666 Fifth Avenue, New York, New York
10103.*

PRINTED IN THE UNITED STATES OF AMERICA

0 9 8 7 6 5 4 3 2 1

One

Frost had silvered the round Somerset hills during the night, and Coralie looked out from her window entranced as the February sun spread pale fingers of light across the garden and white-rimed trees beyond.

Quickly she slipped into her dressing-gown and went downstairs to put the kettle on, hardly noticing the raw chill of the morning because she was listening for the postman, as she always did. "Please, please," she begged silently, "let there be a reply today to one of my applications for a job!"

Three letters dropped to the mat as she carried the tray through the hall, and she took them upstairs with her. "Morning, *Maman*. Tea, and your mail." Smiling, Coralie switched on the lamp.

Mrs. Dee sat up quickly, a small, fragile woman who looked lost in the middle of the big double bed. "Oh, thank you, *chérie*." She took the cup of tea and sipped it with every appearance of enjoyment, which was quite a feat, thought Coralie, knowing her life-long preference for coffee. But as her strong-willed mother had decreed that they should cut down on coffee when money became tight four years ago, she wasn't going to argue.

"Mail, did you say?" Mrs. Dee asked. "Anything interesting?"

Coralie handed her an air-mail letter. "The usual from *Tante* Elise, and what looks like the gas bill." Then she paused, turning over the third envelope curiously. "This one's for me—from North York-shire. Oh—I expect it's an application form for that job. You remember, the one with the box number."

Almost reluctantly she started to open it. "This will be the eighteenth, so far," she said, managing a smile but inwardly dreading the same old perfor-mance once again. Like many recently qualified students Coralie was having difficulty in finding a job. Five times so far she had been in contention, but each time had been beaten by more experienced candidates.

"Come on, pet, see who it's from." Mrs. Dee thumped an extra pillow into place behind her and snuggled further inside a woolly wrap. She spoke in French, her native tongue, but Coralie didn't notice. They both slipped constantly from French to En-glish, with the result that Coralie had grown up speaking both languages with equal ease.

She opened the envelope. "Good heavens! It's from Scarlett's! You know—Scarlett Textiles." Quickly she scanned the form and the accompanying letter. "Why on earth should a firm like that have used a box number?"

"So that competitors don't get to know all their business, I suppose," suggested Mrs. Dee sensibly. Then, after a moment, she looked across at her daughter and said thoughtfully, "But do they have competitors? I always thought Scarlett's were in a class of their own."

Coralie's mercurial spirits soared. "They're terrif-ic!" Her eyes, clear hazel in colour, looked almost amber for a moment in the light of the lamp. "Do you remember that gorgeous blue suit you made for Mrs. Johnson last year—wasn't that a Scarlett tweed? And that display we saw in Bridgewater—co-ordinated patterns and plains, weren't they Scar-lett's as well?"

"Yes, yes," agreed her mother, "but they're textiles, Coralie. Where do you come in with fashion design? Did they ask for a designer of clothes or of textiles?"

"Clothes, of course. I'm certain of it. 'Experienced designer up-market ladies' fashions, used to working on own initiative,' all that stuff. Not that it described me exactly, but then, whoever does advertise for an inexperienced designer?"

"You are more talented than any of them, experienced or not!" declared Mrs. Dee with sweeping maternal loyalty. "Now, off you go if you want first turn in the shower, or I'll be late for work."

Coralie put the empty cups on the tray and gave her mother a quick kiss. "If all those prospective employers had shared your faith in me I'd have been offered a job long ago," she said ruefully, "and then you wouldn't have needed to go out to work. Oh, I know it's only two days a week, but I'd be much happier if you didn't have to turn out in the mornings—you know as well as I do that if we hadn't had such a dry winter your chest would have been playing up weeks ago."

Francine Dee jumped out of bed and faced her daughter, her dark eyes bright and determined. "Hurry along, *chérie*," she said lightly. "I've told you before that I'm perfectly able to cope, especially with you back home again."

Coralie went to the bathroom, pinned her long, heavy blonde hair firmly on top of her head and covered it completely with a shower cap, groaning inwardly as she thought about her job at the supermarket, the "temporary" job which was fast becoming too permanent for her liking. The girls were friendly and she got on well with them, but sometimes she felt that another day at the busy check-out would send her completely and dramatically insane.

For the next eight days she hardly dared hope that she would be granted an interview with Scarlett's. Each morning she caught the village bus into the town, and on Tuesday, which was market day, and Saturday which was equally busy, Mrs. Dee went with her. On those mornings Coralie realised anew that the hours in the elegant little shop were as good as a tonic to her mother. In fact, if it had not been for the ever-present problem of Mrs. Dee's health, Coralie would have been content to see her working there full-time, rather than toiling at home for endless hours over the sewing machine.

Two more refusals of jobs had arrived for Coralie since she applied to Scarlett's.

She told herself that she was daunted but undeterred; or did she mean deterred but undaunted? She thought with some unease about her application to Scarlett's. There had been the usual list of "qualifications to date"—O levels and A levels, which, fortunately in her case, were above average. Then she had been able to mention her excellent results at the end of the design course, and her prizewinning set of designs in the final year. And that was all! No practical experience to boast about apart from the clothes she had designed and made up at college.

All applicants had been asked to send in an original design for a ladies' outdoor garment which would lend itself to being made up in a loose-woven tweed material. She had sent off a detailed sketch of a swirly thigh-length cape with a diagonal fastening and a little peaked cap to match. It was a design she had thought about for some time, young and dashing, but quite suitable for an older woman provided she had a certain sense of style.

That done, she had gone further and specified the exact material for the garment, a willow-green tweed. She had seen it in a small, expensive shop which regularly stocked Scarlett fabrics. . . .

Coralie thought about that design as her register rang and clashed interminably. It would look good with a yellow sweater similar to the one she had just bought, but had she been right in deciding on trousers for the outfit? Yes, she felt sure that a slim, long-legged line would be right. Perhaps she should

4

have specified the fabric for those as well? They would look marvellous in that plain, close-woven wool—the one with the smooth, almost silky finish. . . .

On the ninth day a letter came from Scarlett's, and once again Coralie opened it over the early-morning tea. It was polite, brief, and to the point, asking her to interview at 4 p.m. on Wednesday of the following week, in Mr. Scarlett's suite at the Dorchester Hotel, Park Lane, London. Miss Dee would be applicant number 15, and would she please bring with her a folio of her recent designs? All expenses incurred by her for travelling, meals, etc., would of course be reimbursed on the spot.

The signature of the Chairman and Managing Director was in a forceful, legible hand. J.J. Scarlett. It looked as if the job was an important one, if the top man himself was interviewing applicants.

Coralie did a little war dance around the bedroom, beaming at her mother and waving the letter aloft. Her hair, in its thick night-time plait, still swayed slightly when she stopped, suddenly serious. "The Dorchester!" she said in awe. "What shall I wear?" The thought of entering that elegant establishment in the patterned blanket-cloth coat, which was her current winter outift, somehow failed to appeal.

Mrs. Dee looked up at her daughter, tall and blonde like her late father, but with the faintly golden skin bestowed by her French blood. She wasn't beautiful, she wasn't even pretty in the obvious, accepted sense of the word, but she was lovely with the loveliness which comes from a generous nature and that, partnered by fine bone structure, radiant good health and her very unusual colouring, made her an extremely attractive young woman. A young woman who deserved to arrive at the Dorchester suitably dressed, decided her mother.

"We will make the green cape, of course," she announced, as if stating the obvious. "We know that

5

the cloth is available in town. You can draft the pattern and cut it out, and then together we will sew it."

"*Maman*!" Coralie was impressed, but dubious. "It will be horribly expensive. How could we afford it?"

Mrs. Dee had the grace to blush. "I have a small sum put away which I haven't mentioned when we have been working out our budget," she admitted. "I wanted to save it for something special—like this."

"You don't think it will look as if I'm—presumptuous, or—or pushing?" asked Coralie, rather wary of such blatant tactics at her interview.

"Certainly not! It will show you have drive, flair, and initiative," said Francine Dee, lifting her wrist in a dismissive gesture. The matter was settled in that raising of a small, capable hand.

And so the willow-green tweed was bought; fine smooth cloth in the same colour for the trousers and lining for the cape, a daffodil yellow to match Coralie's new sweater. The total cost caused Coralie some heart-searching, but no concern at all as to the success of the finished ensemble. She knew her own capabilities, and equally important, her mother's skill with the needle, for hadn't she trained in one of the great *couture* houses of Paris until events in 1940 cut short that exacting apprenticeship?

Together they worked on the outfit, until by the evening before the interview it was almost finished. Coralie assembled her latest designs, along with several conceived specially for Scarlett fabrics, while Francine sewed the hem of the trousers with loose, invisible stitches.

When Coralie wore the finished ensemble next morning she stalked up and down the living-room in a fair imitation of a haughty model on the cat-walk. Then she gave Francine a boisterous hug and a kiss. "Thank you, *Maman*. I couldn't possibly have done it without you," she said gratefully.

"It has turned out well, and the material is wonderful," acknowledged Francine with a smile. "Go on, off you go, and the very best of luck."

Coralie leaned forward in her seat as the train slowed and then stopped just outside Paddington. In spite of all her resolves she was feeling nervous and on edge. She wondered how many people would interview her. Would it be a panel—seven or eight experts all firing questions at her? No, more likely two or three people from the design department, and of course, the terse and business-like J.J. Scarlett himself. She could picture him quite clearly. Fiftyish, stout, and balding; with a plain no-nonsense Yorkshire accent, one of these "I'm a self-made man" types.

With renewed misgivings she stared down at the willow green trousers, which were tucked into the tops of her cream leather boots; then she transferred her gaze to the cape, folded carefully on the luggage rack above her head. Surely she looked all wrong for an interview with a solid, old-fashioned firm like Scarlett's.

At last the train pulled in, and she became part of the jostling, pushing crowd approaching the barrier. She would have to take a taxi—or she might actually be late, and that was too awful to even think about! Hastily she joined the queue, her nose wrinkling at the petrol fumes. London was fantastic, of course, it was just that at first you missed the sweet, countryside smell of home.

Then she noticed a barrow loaded with spring flowers, and impulsively bought a bunch of primroses. They would be a sort of mascot—a good-luck token.

"The Dorchester," she said self-consciously when a moment later it was her turn and she boarded a taxi. She placed her folio carefully on the seat at her side, aware that she felt much better since buying the primroses. Odd, and no doubt crazy, but still . . .

7

At three fifty-five, Coralie reached the Scarlett suite, having had time for no more than a rapid tidy-up in the ladies' room before taking the lift. Her freshly-shampooed hair was tidy now, hanging straight and shining well below her shoulder-blades, and the little green cap was set upon it at a confident angle. She took a deep breath and went in.

Four people were sitting in a small ante-room which apparently was serving as a waiting room. Were they all waiting to go in before her? If so, she needn't have rushed like a maniac.

A plump, composed woman with grey hair took Coralie's name, and asking for her folio of designs pressed on to it a small sticker which said, simply, "Miss Dee, No. 15." "Please take a seat, Miss Dee," she said pleasantly, and carried off the folio to the next room.

Coralie sat down, looking with interest at the other candidates. At once her heart sank. They were all older than she was, and—oh no, it couldn't be! But it was. The dark-haired woman in the crimson bat-wing coat was Myra Bergson, who had judged the third-year design competition at college. Judged it! And the two men—they both looked well over thirty; one was an arty, perpetual-student type and the other the absolute opposite, precise and bespectacled, like the popular image of an accountant or solicitor. They both seemed confident and rather bored by the whole affair.

It was almost four, but Coralie felt she could relax a little. If she came after the others she could take a breather.

"Miss Dee? This way, please."

Coralie shot to her feet, astonished. The others must have arrived early for their appointments. Her new-found calm deserted her. She dropped her handbag, picked it up, and clutched the primroses in a vice-like grip, wondering why on earth she'd been idiot enough to buy them in the first place.

Then she walked as elegantly as her wobbly knees would allow into the next room.

"Miss Dee. Number 15," announced the grey-haired woman, and then went out and shut the door.

One man was in the room, standing by the windows overlooking a rain-washed Hyde Park. Just one man. Coralie glanced around nervously, and couldn't help feeling slightly cheated after her visions of a panel of seven or eight razor-sharp Yorkshiremen. Her collection of designs were spread out on a large polished table, but she paid them scant attention, standing tensely just inside the door and looking at the man by the window. She saw that he was not fiftyish, stout and balding as she had pictured; but thirtyish, lean and muscular, with thick dark hair. To complete the full list of her mistaken preconceptions, his voice when he spoke was deep, cultured, and with only the faintest trace of the hard Northern inflection.

"Good afternoon," he said, coming towards her. "I'm Jethro Scarlett."

"Good afternoon." She risked a smile. A mere weak travesty of her usual one, but even so his eyes widened slightly as if in surprise when they shook hands. Perhaps the majority of candidates didn't smile at all? His handclasp was firm, warm, and brief, and she saw that in his left hand he held her sketch of the green cape.

"I see you are wearing your design," he said thoughtfully. "Would you please walk up and down for a moment?"

Coralie swallowed. She might have expected this, of course. If she chose to wear her own creation then she shouldn't be surprised at having to perform like a model. She laid her bag and the primroses carefully on the table and obediently walked a few steps in either direction.

"Mm. Now, Miss Dee. Would you be good enough

to remove the cape and let me see your trousers?"

Colour mounted swiftly to her cheeks, but with no other visible sign of dismay she unbuttoned the cape, swung it from her shoulders, and passed it over to his outstretched hand. Once again she walked, turned, and came back, her cheeks pink. She felt that there was an almost nightmare unreality about the proceedings. Thank goodness that at least she hadn't got a fat bottom or a bulging midriff to exhibit.

"Thank you," said Jethro Scarlett impassively.

She stood in front of him again as he examined the cape closely, turning it inside out, feeling the weight of it, and fingering the cunning little loops which fitted round each domed button.

After a moment he lifted his head, and taking a step forward laid the cape gently around her shoulders, lifting her hair out of the way with firm, impersonal fingers. Then he placed a chair in front of the table for her and seated himself at the opposite side.

"Now," he said briskly. "Let's get down to it."

She waited expectantly, unnerved when he said nothing at all for a moment, but just looked intently into her face. With an effort she gathered her wits and studied him just as curiously, impressed in spite of herself by the startlingly vivid blue eyes under straight black brows, and the wide, unsmiling mouth. It was a serious face, and rather handsome, with an alert, arresting expression which did nothing to quiet the butterflies in her stomach.

And then she saw he was half-smiling, revealing very white teeth, one of which was slightly crooked. "What's the matter?" he asked. "Didn't you enjoy displaying your wares?"

His choice of words could have been deliberate or just accidental. To Coralie's heightened sensibilities, it sounded as if he referred to the display of her figure, for she had certainly been conscious that the well-cut trousers and tight-fitting sweater had left little to the imagination.

"I should have expected it," she said stiffly, and saw his smile disappear abruptly.

He looked at her application form. "You are without experience since college, I see. You did notice that we asked particularly for an experienced designer?"

"Yes, of course. But how does one get to be experienced? I mean, if nobody will employ you in the first place?"

He made no reply, and she wriggled uneasily in her seat. She was off to a bad start. Then she found the vivid blue gaze on her again. "Miss Dee, did it occur to you to wonder why a textile firm should advertise for a fashion designer?"

"Yes, it did. I surmised that you wanted fashion designs for advertisements for your fabrics—something like that."

"No. It's bigger than that. Scarlett's are going into ready-to-wear. We're going to sell by mail-order. Top-grade ladies' fashions, straight from the mill, made in Scarlett fabrics."

Coralie's self-consciousness disappeared at that. She fixed her clear, tawny gaze on Jethro Scarlett's face and listened attentively.

"This isn't new, of course. Other firms have done it, and still do, very successfully. We shall do it better and bigger, that's all."

The underlying note of assurance in that remark, the confidence of it, was impressive. She listened closely.

"We want a single designer to have overall responsibility for the whole collection. Does that interest you?"

"Very much," said Coralie, even as her hopes sank lower. She really hadn't a chance. The job would probably go to Myra Bergson, sitting out there looking so capable and elegant and—and unruffled.

"We will issue a well-produced catalogue offering a limited number of designs in a wide range of colours and sizes. Does that suggest anything to you?"

Hesitantly, Coralie said: "It suggests—very careful design in the first instance."

"Well—naturally." J.J. Scarlett raised immaculately clad shoulders in the suggestion of a shrug, then pushed back a spotless cuff and glanced at his watch. Obviously he had hoped for a more enterprising reply, so she tried again.

"Clean simple lines, nothing too trendy. Classics that won't date by the next season. Mail-order could mean customers in country districts; and upper middle-class, I should think, if I gauge your prices correctly. Well-off country-dwellers quite often buy good quality clothes which don't date too easily, with maybe a little high fashion for evenings and the odd grand occasion."

Consideringly he looked at her. "Mm," he said. "If you wanted to advertise this collection, where would you do it?"

"The quality dailies and Sunday papers, glossies . . ."

"Mm," he said once more, causing Coralie to smother a nervous and maybe slightly hysterical giggle. If he said it again she would scream.

"What do you think is the motive behind all this?" he asked.

Against her will Coralie's gaze strayed around the sumptuous room where they were sitting.

"Profit," she replied bluntly.

But Jethro Scarlett had not missed her quick look at their surroundings and had interpreted it correctly.

"All this," he said, waving a large hand at the room, "is just a drop in the ocean. It's a convenient place to interview applicants in comfort. But much more important, I've taken these rooms in order to entertain customers later today, after I have finished the business of deciding who gets this position. Normally I wouldn't be doing it single-handed, even though design is a special interest of mine, but today circumstances decreed otherwise."

She remained silent, and he went on, "No, the reason for this new departure is to promote Scarlett materials, to compete in a wider field, and to keep our present work-force in full employment without sacrificing the high quality of our cloth. If the venture succeeds, we will make a profit. If not, we will sustain a loss. It's as simple as that. Now, Miss Dee. The successful applicant will have to live in Yorkshire—in Raxby. Are you prepared to do that if necessary?"

"Yes, of course."

"Good. Do you have any—attachments or commitments which could make it awkward to live away from—" he consulted his notes—"Somerset?"

"My only close relative is my mother, whose health isn't too good, but she accepts and approves the fact that I will have to move away from home for a job in design."

"I see; and can you take pressure? Pressure on the job? At Scarlett's there would be deadlines to meet, one-off models to be designed and made up for approval, sometimes very quickly. Could you cope with that?"

"I'm not sure," she turned her wide golden gaze on him, frowning slightly," "but I'd certainly try."

"Who made your outfit?" he asked abruptly. "You?"

"No, not entirely. My mother helped me. She trained in *haute couture* in Paris when she was young."

"It's beautifully made. What do you think of the cloth?"

"It's lovely. I've always admired your material," she said with complete honesty.

"Did you send in that particular design because you had already made the outfit and knew it looked good?"

"Oh no," she said quickly, slightly shocked at the idea. "I wouldn't have made it up at all if I hadn't been offered this interview."

He lifted his head and she thought she saw the shadow of disbelief in his eyes. "I wouldn't normally buy anything so expensive," she explained, reluctant to labour the point that she wasn't rolling in money.

He let that go, glancing at his watch again. "I'm sorry about the number 15 that's attached to you," he said. "Once, long ago, two Mr. Robinsons applied for the same job. By mistake it was offered to the wrong one, so ever since, as a precaution, all applicants have a number as well as a name. You're the last candidate anyway, did you realise that?"

"But—there are four more out there."

"I've seen them all. They're waiting for the verdict—I have to make a final decision this afternoon. Will you please go and join them for a few minutes? That's if there's nothing you'd like to ask me first?"

Puzzled, she rose from her chair and faced him as he came round the table. At closer quarters she could see that his skin was smooth and fine-textured for a man, with a dark shadow of beard already showing around the hard jaw-line.

He looked weary and a trifle put-out when she didn't reply at once. "Salary," he said patiently, enunciating slowly as if to a child. "Don't you want to know how much we're offering for the job? You realise that it's a responsible position, I take it?"

"Yes. I can see that quite clearly. I suppose I should have asked. How much?"

"Five thousand pounds, plus accommodation. But for someone who preferred to find a place of their own to live we would increase to, say, five thousand eight hundred."

Coralie stared at him.

It was far beyond anything she could possibly hope to earn as an inexperienced twenty-one-year-old. And if she wasn't going to get the job she would have been happier not knowing what she had missed.

"I see. Thank you," she said quietly, and turned to pick up her bag and the primroses, but Jethro Scarlett was already handing them to her. He put the cool little flowers into her hand, stood back and eyed her once again, then said: "Very effective. The perfect finishing touch, in fact."

For a few seconds she didn't follow his meaning, but the implication was obvious. He was telling her that he knew she had carried the primroses purely for effect.

Forgetting all her resolutions about being courteous and respectful Coralie glared up at him. Why should she let him get away with it? She clutched the primroses to her chest defensively and said slowly and distinctly, "I bought them on impulse at the station, as a mascot. I might have known what was facing me, mightn't I?"

She saw surprise on the dark features, and—surely it was a hint of amusement, quickly suppressed? Then she turned and went out to join the others, in what she hoped was a dignified manner.

The friendly redhead looked at her expectantly, but Coralie just smiled bleakly, and kept silent. That was that, she thought wearily. What a long way to come for nothing.

There was silence and a growing tension among those waiting; even the redhead looked subdued and apprehensive. Twenty minutes passed, during which only one point of any interest became apparent to Coralie. The other four all had their design folios with them, while hers was still in there, with Jethro Scarlett.

All at once the door opened and he stood there, tall and impressive in the suit of classic dark-blue worsted; made, presumably, from his own cloth.

"Miss Dee, would you come in again, please?"

She walked past him and into the room, and he turned towards her before going out again. "I won't keep you a moment," he said shortly.

Edgily she paced the soft carpet, and then went to the window and looked out. Down below the traffic surged along Park Lane, and the Park itself, rain-swept and deserted, looked alien and other-worldly amid the tumult surrounding it. She realised suddenly that the poor little primroses were being crushed in her tense grip, and she lifted them gently to her cheek in silent apology. Then the door opened again.

"Congratulations, Miss Dee. The job's yours, if you want it," said Jethro Scarlett. And with that he came and stood opposite her by the window, his hand outstretched, his expression guarded and just a little bit uneasy.

Two

Afterwards Coralie found it difficult to recall the next half-hour in any sort of sequence. She could remember her astonishment, first at his words, and then at the way he seemed to be waiting to see if she would accept the job, as if he by no means thought it a foregone conclusion. And then his sudden smile, brilliant and astonishingly attractive. . . .

"I felt such an idiot, *Maman*," she said late that night when she regaled Francine with a detailed account of all that had happened. "I was so thrilled I grabbed his hand in both of mine, when obviously all he had expected was a handshake to seal the bargain. He looked irritated, like someone does when a puppy is being a nuisance.

"Then, knowing I'd arrived straight from the station, he asked if I'd had lunch on the train, and I said just a sandwich, and he looked irritated again, and rang room service and ordered me a cooked meal, at half past four in the afternoon, and it came in silver dishes, with all the trimmings, and it was gorgeous. Until it arrived we talked, and of course all that made me miss the five-twenty, and that's why I missed the last bus from town."

"Did he confirm the salary?" asked Francine, always practical.

Coralie, who had been lying back in her chair, leaned forward to give full weight to her next bit of information. "He said I hadn't looked too enthusiastic about the salary, and was it satisfactory? I

17

nearly fainted on the spot, and said yes, it was quite satisfactory, thank you. Then he looked astonished! Perhaps he expected me to try for more, I don't know. And then he just said, 'I'm offering you a bonus of an extra thousand as a lump sum if the catalogue is a success.'

"And then—I think I'll just have that last sandwich, *Maman*—and then he asked how soon I could start; and when I said I would have to give a week's notice at Benson's, he said would they have trouble replacing me? When I said no, on the contrary, he just told me to forfeit a week's wages in lieu of notice and wrote a cheque to cover it, and then gave me my fare up to Yorkshire as well. I'm to travel up on Saturday and start on Monday."

She looked at her mother with an expression almost of dismay. "Did you ever hear of such a quick worker? I don't know if I'm on my head or my heels. I simply can't believe it."

"You say settle on Sunday? But where?"

"There's a converted coach-house available, all furnished and everything."

Francine tried to sound casual. "Where is this coach-house?"

Coralie looked at her fondly. "It's all right. Don't go getting silly ideas. It's a self-contained flat over what is now a garage, but was originally a coach-house. Mr. Scarlett said he'll make sure his housekeeper sees that it's warm and ready for me."

"But why couldn't you live in a flat in the town in the usual way?"

"Because at his house he has a studio which I can use, if at any time I want to work there instead of at the mill."

"He sounds as if he's extremely pleased to get you," observed Francine, unable to conceal a note of maternal pride. "What sort of man is he?"

Coralie thought for a moment before replying. "He's younger than I expected—early to mid-thirties, I should say. Clever, bossy, a bit ruthless. One of these human dynamo types. And he isn't bald, either," she added sleepily, rather to her mother's perplexity.

With that Francine had to be content, for Coralie, with a gigantic yawn, kissed her goodnight and went off to bed. But her mother sat on in the lamplight, looking at a silver-framed photograph on the small table at her side. The eyes of the middle-aged man in the picture were a clear, striking hazel; and after a while, as if finding reassurance in their depths, Francine smiled gently to herself, switched off the lamp, and followed her daughter up the stairs.

Almost three days to the hour after her interview with Jethro Scarlett, Coralie was once more travelling by train at his bidding, but this time up through North Yorkshire on the branch line to Raxby.

Her employer had warned her to be prepared for colder weather than she was used to in Somerset, a show of concern on his part which she had appreciated, even while thinking it unnecessary. Did he imagine she didn't know that it would be colder nearly three hundred miles further north? Even so, when she changed trains at York, she had been shocked at the icy blast of wind along the platforms, and was glad of her hooded blanket-cloth coat, inadequate though it suddenly seemed.

Now the train was slowing for Raxby and she hurriedly gathered her belongings together. She travelled light—for the simple reason that she hadn't enough clothes to do otherwise, and her record-player and records had been left behind until later.

She stepped out on to the platform, remembering Jethro Scarlett's promise that she would be met, and almost immediately saw the now-familiar figure of his secretary, Miss Silverwood, the grey-haired woman she had last seen at the Dorchester.

"Lovely to see you, Miss Dee," she said now, cheerfully. "Right on time as well. Mr. Scarlett has asked me to take you straight to your flat. The car's just outside." Then she looked round in surprise. "But where is the rest of your luggage?"

"It's all here," said Coralie, indicating one suitcase and a tote. "It's awfully good of you to give up your free time on a Saturday like this."

Miss Silverwood laughed as she led Coralie out of the little station. "Working for Mr. Scarlett isn't a nine-till-five job, you know—and I wouldn't want it to be; I like a bit of variety." She put the case in the back of a large estate car, and said, as if in answer to a question, "This is Mr. Scarlett's car. He told me to use it, as he thought all your gear might be too much for my Mini, but he needn't have worried, need he?"

Coralie couldn't imagine anybody less likely to worry than Jethro Scarlett, but naturally she kept this opinion to herself. She had noticed at the Dorchester that a very real liking and mutual respect seemed to exist between the woman at her side and her employer.

Curious, she looked out as they sped through Raxby. It was almost dark, but to her surprise she could see little evidence of a busy industrial town. Most of the houses were built of stone, and nearly all of them had gardens. Here and there a field or stretch of open ground gave an uninterrupted view of great hills curving upwards to the dark, cloud-torn sky.

"Aren't we in Raxby yet?" she asked, puzzled.

"We've just come through it," said her companion. "It's no more than a large village, you know, providing just about half the workforce at the mill. The rest either have their own transport or come in from elsewhere on special buses. In a minute now we'll be passing the mill, but you will hardly see it as it's almost dark."

A moment later she slowed the car. "Look—down there," she said, indicating the valley on their right.

But though Coralie peered intently through the fading light she could see little beyond the outline of a large building, and then they turned off the road up a narrow lane edged by low stone walls.

"This is the road up to Mr. Scarlett's house, Raxhead, where his family have lived for generations," said Miss Silverwood. "It's about half a mile from the mill, with a lovely view over the valley. I'm taking you to the house itself, so that Mr. Scarlett's housekeeper can take you across to your flat."

In the beam of the headlights Coralie saw a great, stone-built house with a wide frontage overlooking the valley, and smooth sweeps of lawn curving down to a narrow lane which went off into the distance across the face of the hill. One or two of the tall windows glowed with light, the rest were in darkness.

"Is—is Mr. Scarlett at home?" asked Coralie, not feeling in the least like meeting the human dynamo himself just then.

"No, he'll be back later. He's gone to Leeds on business today. As I said, there's no such thing as nine-till-five and a five-day week with Mr. Scarlett."

When Coralie met Mrs. Braithwaite, the housekeeper, she noticed at once the strong likeness between her and Miss Silverwood, the only difference being another thirty pounds or so of dimpled flesh distributed around the person of the housekeeper.

Both women laughed. "We're sisters," explained Miss Silverwood. "Practically everyone in the valley is either related, or employed by Scarlett's, or both."

For some reason this reassured Coralie, who said a grateful goodbye to her and followed the other woman across an open, windswept courtyard to her flat.

She was intrigued to see that access to it was outside the building, by means of a stout wooden staircase with open treads. "Watch this. You could have a nasty fall when the weather's bad," Mrs.

21

Braithwaite pointed out, quite as if the gale howling around them was an example of weather that was good.

She opened the door. "Here you are then, here's your key, and I have a spare one in case you lock yourself out." Then she marched inside and proceeded to open doors at random. "Bedroom, bath-room, kitchen, and this is your living-room."

"But it's gorgeous," cried Coralie, staring at the white painted walls and steeply pitched roof of dark, criss-crossed timbers. "It's really lovely, and thank you for getting it ready for me."

A satisfied smile was allowed to rest on Mrs. Braithwaite's plump features for a moment. "I don't say it wasn't a rush—changing the bedroom round and everything, but Walter—that's my husband—he's like greased lightning when Mr. Scarlett asks him to do anything." A certain light in her eye hinted that Walter was just the opposite when asked to do something for his wife. "Your food cupboard is well-stocked, and your fridge," she said, moving to the door. "Mr. Scarlett was most particular about me doing that."

"Oh, was he? How kind," Coralie said, taken aback. "But who shall I pay for the food? You?"

"See Mr. Scarlett. He didn't tell me to charge you for anything. Now, I've left you a nice casserole in the oven so help yourself, and if there's anything I've forgotten, or anything you want to know, I shall be in the house all evening, and all tomorrow until tea-time, so just come across."

With that comforting remark, she departed, leaving Coralie to explore her new domain. It was beautifully warm, and she saw that radiators heated each room, with an electric fire as well in the living-room. The floor was of broad golden boards, and there were a few exceptionally lovely rugs in glowing jewel colours. On impulse she turned one back. Yes, there was the wool mark, surmounted by a twist of scarlet thread and the words 'Scarlett of Raxby.' So they made rugs as well, did they?

The bathroom and kitchen were beautifully equipped; and, as for the bedroom—what had Mrs. Braithwaite meant by her remark about changing it round? The room was right under the sloping eaves of the coach-house, with fitted white cupboards, a scrolly cane headboard to the bed and a continental quilt in a pretty pink and white patchwork design. The floor was covered in deep pink shag-pile carpet.

It was marvellous. She was the luckiest girl on earth, she told herself as she sat at the neatly-laid table enjoying the beef casserole. And everyone was so kind! Even Jethro Scarlett himself had apparently gone out of his way to make her welcome.

Then she thought of the two women she had met so far, and decided that if the staff at Scarlett's were half as friendly as they were, then she couldn't help but be happy working there. And how wrong she had been in imagining it to be a gigantic concern engaged in cut-throat business tactics. From what Miss Silverwood had said it sounded more like an old-established family firm, and the idea of that was somehow reassuring. After all, just because Jethro Scarlett acted like a big-business tycoon it didn't necessarily mean he controlled an industrial empire.

Feeling delighted with her new home and extraordinarily pleased with the way things were turning out, Coralie washed the dishes, marvelling anew at the trim dark-blue and white kitchen. Then she put on her coat and boots and a long woolly scarf for good measure. She had noticed a phone booth as they left the main road, so she would brave the tempest to go and ring her mother with reassurances that she was safe and sound.

The lane was steeper than she had thought, but at least she was going downhill as she faced the full onslaught of the north-easterly gale. Her hitherto

23

warm coat felt like a useless rag around her, and she clutched at her hood and scarf in an effort to keep her throat and ears from freezing.

She was nearing the road itself, head down, when she was caught in the sweeping beam of headlights. With a screech of brakes a car stopped just a few feet in front of her and the door slammed as the driver jumped out.

She sensed who it would be before he spoke. It seemed she was not going to escape him on her first evening after all.

"What on earth are you doing down here?" he bellowed crossly. "Good grief, girl, I thought you'd be settled in by now. What's wrong?"

Coralie gaped at him as she clutched her scarf and re-wound it several times around her neck. She replied with some difficulty as the wind knocked the words back into her throat. "Nothing is wrong, Mr. Scarlett. I'm on my way to the phone booth to ring my mother."

"Oh, for goodness' sake! Why didn't you telephone from the house? Didn't it occur to you?"

"No," said Coralie honestly. "But thanks, anyway," and with that she edged past him and trudged the few remaining yards to the phone.

"Are you sure everything is all right?" asked Francine a minute later, her sensitive ear having registered a trace of agitation in her daughter's voice.

"Yes, don't worry, *Maman*. The flat is beautiful. The journey was fine. I've had a lovely supper and I'm going to have a hot bath and an early night. I'll ring you on Monday to tell you about my first day at work. Yes—everyone is very kind and very pleasant."

Everyone except Jethro Scarlett, she amended silently. Then she turned back into the lane. "Girl" indeed! Had he forgotten already that she had a name?

But the low-slung car was still there, where he had

stopped so abruptly when he saw her. "Get in," he said, leaning across and opening the door.

"I'm sorry, I didn't realise you were waiting," she said a trifle breathlessly, slipping into the seat at his side.

He started up the slope without replying, and she found herself still shivering with cold as she looked across at him. "The flat is absolutely lovely, Mr. Scarlett," she said earnestly. "I can't tell you how delighted I am with it . . ."

"Then don't try," he advised promptly.

"But—I mean—it's centrally heated but I can't find a boiler, or a meter, or anything. Do I pay you for heating? And who must I pay for all the food Mrs. Braithwaite has bought for me? I'm sorry to bother you with all these domestic details, but you see, I didn't expect to find so much laid on for me."

He pulled up in front of the garage, switched on the light inside the car and looked at her intently, his eyes seeming much darker than she remembered. She thought he looked tired and rather impatient, but when he spoke his deep voice was surprisingly gentle.

"I quite realise that you wish to be independent and to live without interference or any kind of supervision. I will see that your wishes in this are respected. Your central heating boiler is in the garage here. It is powered from the house and runs at my expense. What is more, I am not quite destitute, and can afford a bag of sugar or the odd packet of tea without going bankrupt. I can also afford to pay for your phone calls—so please don't go down to the main road in all weathers, and alone, just to telephone your mother, or anyone else for that matter."

He came round and opened the car door for her. "And another thing before you go. Get rid of that rubbishy coat. It's useless for early March in this part of the world. I did warn you to bring some warm clothes, you know."

Coralie shivered again, and clenched her jaw tightly to prevent her teeth from chattering. Did he think she had an unlimited supply of warm coats to choose from?

"Go on," he said. "Get indoors before you turn into an icicle."

Suddenly, humiliatingly, she felt her lower lip tremble. Need he be such a horror? Without a word she went past him, and climbed the steps to her flat.

Shortly afterwards, while soaking in a blissfully hot bath, she found she could almost smile at the memory of that little scene. Financially she would be better off than she could ever have expected, and she knew that she must count her blessings.

The doorbell rang just as she was drying herself. Hastily she grabbed her brief towelling robe and slipped it on. Mrs. Braithwaite must have come across for something. She ran to the door, anxious not to keep her waiting on the exposed landing at the top of the stairs, but it was Jethro Scarlett who stood there, the wind whipping his heavy dark hair across his forehead.

When he saw she was wearing only a bathrobe he groaned. "I can see you're going all-out to catch pneumonia! Could I just step inside for a moment to shut out the wind?"

Warily she stood back as he came in and closed the door, experiencing a fleeting sense of satisfaction when she saw that he looked ill at ease as he eyed her flushed cheeks and the damp tendrils of hair which had escaped when she pinned it up.

"I'm sorry to arrive at your door so soon after I'd assured you that you'd be left alone, Miss Dee," he said stiffly, "but I wondered if you are free tomorrow afternoon, and if so, whether you'd like me to show you over the mill? I'm just on my way out, and thought I would mention it now, so that you can plan your day."

She saw then that he was in evening dress

beneath his thick coat. Goodness, the man had only been in the house twenty minutes and here he was, all set to go dashing off again. She noticed that he was carefully avoiding her eyes now, or was he maybe staring at her bare legs, which were still slightly pink from the bath?

It suddenly seemed important to put him at his ease. "That will be lovely," she agreed, with her wide and truly beautiful smile. "What time shall I go to the mill?"

"I'll be ready at two," he said, "I'll take you down."

But Coralie wasn't too happy about that, and when she wasn't happy about something she usually said so. "It's very kind of you, Mr. Scarlett, but I really don't expect you to be giving me lifts up and down the hill all the time, just because I live up here near you."

Glittering blue eyes looked impatiently into clear tawny ones, and she wondered why she had imagined him to be ill at ease. "I didn't think you expected anything of the sort," he said. "Quite the reverse, in fact. But if ever we find ourselves going to or from the mill at the same time, you mustn't expect me to sail past in the car and leave you trudging along the lane."

Oh well—he was being reasonable and she was not—she might as well admit it. "All right. Thank you." But in spite of aiming at a pleasant tone of voice she knew she sounded stilted and on edge.

It was five a.m. when she awoke from a restless sleep, troubled by wild, impossible dreams in which she was expected to scale vertical rock-faces and swim across swollen rivers. She was snug and warm in bed, but so wide-awake that at last she decided to get up and have a glass of warm milk.

The sound of a car door closing and voices down below caused her to go to the window. A lamp was shining from the porch, and by its light she saw her employer, tall and dark, and at his side a woman in a pale fur coat and with a scarf around her hair. Laughing together, they hurried inside, and the door closed behind them.

Coralie switched on the kitchen light, poured milk into a pan and placed it on the stove. She was annoyed with herself. That must be the last time she peered out so curiously to see what was happening at the house. She wanted to live without interference, so the least she could do was to have the decency to let Scarlett himself do the same.

She took the milk back to bed and drank it slowly, sitting hugging her knees under the quilt, and from time to time twirling her thick, wheat-coloured plait in her fingers, a habit she had when lost in thought. If J.J. Scarlett wanted to take home female company at five in the morning, what business was it of hers? And for that matter, if she wanted to bring male company up here to her flat at a similar hour, what business was it of his?

The unlikelihood of that happening didn't for a moment occur to her. So, quite pleased with such a line of reasoning, she pulled her hair forward comfortably over her shoulder and snuggled down into the warmth of the bed.

She slept late the next morning and awoke feeling energetic and eager to view her new surroundings in daylight. Hurriedly she washed and dressed and then pulled back the curtains at the large window in the living-room.

The sun shone brilliantly from a clear, cloudless sky, and a gentle breeze played with the branches of a group of firs nearby. Far below, looking small as a child's toy on the floor of the valley, was the mill, and a river shone silver in the sunlight. The mill itself seemed to be built from some sort of light-coloured stone, and Coralie smiled wryly at the thought of her earlier mental picture of it—all blackened brick-work and rows of small, many-paned windows. Wrong again!

Then she studied the great hills across the valley, rolling back in curve after curve up into the high moors. Snow still powdered the highest points, and lower down in the shadowed hollows were the remnants of drifts, unmelted by the last thaw.

The window where she was standing took up almost the whole of the front of the upper floor of the coach-house, and she saw now that it was double-glazed. Just as well, in such an exposed position, she reasoned, but it was yet another instance of the care which had gone into converting the place for some previous occupant. Jethro Scarlett's two-seater was still parked at the front of the house. Perhaps feminine company and the lateness of the hour had decided him against garaging it?

Coralie thought about him as she ate a meal that served as both breakfast and lunch. Perhaps the lady of the fur coat was his wife? Why hadn't she thought of that before?

But thinking back to Mrs. Braithwaite's capable manner, and wholly pleasant type of bossiness, Coralie decided that there was likely to be no mistress up at Raxhead. It was all 'Mr. Scarlett says,' and 'Mr. Scarlett was most particular.' No, as far as she could recall, there had been no mention at all of a Mrs. Scarlett.

And no wonder! In all probability nobody would have him if he was always so rude. "Get rid of that rubbishy coat" indeed! She had a good mind to wear it this afternoon just to show him, although for some absurd reason she felt a bit scared when she thought about a conducted tour of the mill. Not of him, of course! Definitely not. But of something . . . perhaps it was the thought of what she would learn about the responsibilities of her job?

Promptly at two she ran down the staircase, having been on the lookout for Jethro Scarlett crossing the courtyard. She was wearing the green outfit. Not, she told herself, that she was in any way reluctant to wear her blanket-cloth, but because, after all, it was Sunday and he always looked so Savile Row, and the sun was shining. . . .

Yes, the sun was shining, but as she set foot on the landing Coralie realised that although it was spring in Somerset, it was still winter in Yorkshire. The air smelt wonderfully of damp earth and clean moorland, but it was bitterly cold.

She tightened the leather thong beneath her chin and straightened her hat. It was her favourite, bought two summers before when she was on a student camping holiday in Spain. Flat-brimmed and flat-crowned, in dull cream leather. She was wearing it now for the feeling of confidence it gave her. Well—all right, she acknowledged reluctantly, the feeling of confidence it usually gave her.

Scarlett didn't comment on it, but just asked, very pleasantly, if she was settled in quite comfortably, and would she like to see the studio across at the house before they went down to the mill?

"It's always open," he said, "and if you use this entrance you can come and go as you please without bothering the Braithwaites."

She looked round the big square room curiously, noting the drawing board and the easel near the north-facing window, and the open shelves stacked with every kind of design equipment. There was a strange smell in the room, partly oil-paints, and what else?

"Raw wool," he said, accurately reading her thoughts. "I sometimes have a bale or two in here to examine if our buyer wants a second opinion. This used to be the sample room, where my great-grandfather would sort through samples of wool sent in from the shearers, before deciding whether to buy. There was a small hand-loom here as well, at one time, for experimenting with different weaves and colours.

"Now all that is done in the experimental labs at

the mill, and of course you will have full co-operation from that department."

"Oh, good," said Coralie, in what she hoped was a brisk, business-like tone. She looked at the many-coloured skeins of wool hanging from rows of hooks along one wall. "Are these your current colours?"

"Yes." He took down a handful to show her.

She examined them more closely, then walked around the room, weighing up the range of paints and pastels while her companion stood silently, his hands in the pockets of his sheepskin coat. Then she saw, mounted on the wall by the door, a little glass-fronted case containing a twist of faded soft-red wool, wound into a skein.

"What is this, Mr. Scarlett?"

He smiled down at her, much as he had smiled in the luxurious room above Park Lane when she accepted the job. He really should do that more often, thought Coralie. He looks terrific.

"That is a skein of the first wool dyed in Raxby by my family, almost two hundred years ago. The first Scarlett in this valley came from Nottingham, where my ancestors were skilled in the art of dyeing cloth. They came because the sheep in this area were reputed to give superior wool, and that was the beginning of Scarlett's. To this day we still spin and dye all our wools ourselves." He stopped abruptly, and ran lean fingers through his dark hair. "Sorry—I didn't mean to lecture you on family history."

"But it's all so interesting!" said Coralie sincerely. "I think it's wonderful the way you must be able to trace your family back for generations."

"So do I, to be honest, but I don't usually go on about it."

She stood by the door so that he would see she was ready to move on if he wished. Surely he hadn't planned such a leisurely progression? "May I come here to work whenever I like?" she asked.

"Of course. I use it myself occasionally, but not as

often as I would like. It's mainly when we are planning our new season's colours."

"But don't you have a designer for that?" asked Coralie, surprised.

"He's just left us," said Scarlett. "It's his flat you've taken over, as a matter of fact."

Coralie felt as if something very hard had thumped her beneath the ribs. She whirled to face him, nearly losing the leather hat in the process. "But—you don't want me to design your cloth, do you?" she asked quickly, tightening her chin-strap too much and almost choking herself.

"Did I engage you to design cloth?"

"No," she admitted, and then said, without weighing her words, "but you've been very—well—very considerate, and I—I just wondered, that is—I—"

"You wondered if I was softening you up before telling you that I expected you to design textiles as well as fashions?"

"No, of course not! Well, actually . . . yes."

"I think we'd better sort things out, Coralie." He used her name quite as if they'd been on first-name terms for years. "I'm not such a fool as to expect you to know much about textiles, except how to use them for clothes. Right?"

"Right," she agreed in relief.

"And if I've tried to make sure you settle in comfortably it's because I want you to be happy with us. I know that designers are essentially creative, and I have found that creative people are extremely sensitive to environment and atmosphere. A lot depends on your designs, Coralie. The cloth could be marvellous, the models ravishing, the photography brilliant, the catalogue riveting. But if your designs don't hit the right note, don't appeal to a very wide range of women, then the whole venture will be a failure. Is it so very odd that I want you to be content?"

"No, it's very understandable," she admitted flatly, and walked past him as he held the door. "I—I

32

suppose the whole scheme will cost a great deal of money?"

Afterwards she wasn't sure why she had asked, unless she had sought some justification for his generous offer of the bonus.

He descended the stairs behind her. "The last estimate was four hundred thousand," he said, "but I rather think that was on the low side."

Silently she walked at his side to the car, and with a roar of the exhaust they set off down the hill.

Coralie ate her evening meal from a tray on her lap, ostensibly watching television, but actually reviewing the events of the afternoon in the minutest detail. The size of the mill and its adjoining workshops had staggered her, as had Jethro Scarlett's knowledge of each and every process. It had been an illuminating afternoon, touring the empty works in the company of such a knowledgeable guide; and she would have enjoyed every minute, had it not been for the feeling of carrying an intolerable burden the whole time. Four hundred thousand pounds had descended on Coralie's slim shoulders, and by the end of the afternoon she was worn out by the weight of it.

"Do you feel quite well?" asked Scarlett as they left the mill. "You look rather pale."

"Yes, I'm all right." Coralie forced a smile. "Thank you so much for the preview. It's fascinating."

It was quite true. The whole process of manufacturing such high-grade cloth did fascinate her, from the oily, earthy smell of the raw wool right through to the countless fat rolls of finished cloth.

He nodded, apparently only half-convinced, and said little on the way up to Raxhead. "I'll drop in to see you at work tomorrow," he said, "and arrange a meeting of everybody concerned in the new scheme."

Now she took her tray away, still thoughtful. She was warm, well-fed, well-housed and well-paid. She must get down to it and earn her money, suppressing all the multiplying doubts about her own ability. She must show initiative, drive, and flair. Yes, that was what she must do, because it all rested on her; Jethro Scarlett had said so.

She paced up and down the room, twirling the end of her plait, her tie-and-dye caftan swirling around her legs each time she turned. The next moment she was out of the flat and running down the stairs, her skirt held high out of the way. She rang the doorbell of the house, searching for something plausible to say to Mrs. Braithwaite when she opened the door. But it was Scarlett himself who stood there, wearing cream trousers and a fine, sky-blue sweater. "What—why, Coralie! Come in. Is anything wrong? Come into the study—Judith and Walter have gone out, it's a wonder I heard the bell."

He led her into a small, book-lined room. A log fire burned in the hearth, and a big desk was covered with papers, as was the hearth-rug. The haunting music of Sibelius filled the room, but Scarlett crossed to the fitted hi-fi unit and switched it off; then he pulled forward a leather chair. "Sit down, Coralie. Now, is there something worrying you? What's wrong?"

"I want to resign," she blurted out awkwardly. "I'm truly sorry, but I don't think I can do it. I'm frightened I'll lose all the money you're putting into the new project."

Three

When the words were out she avoided his eyes, unwilling to face the scorn and anger which she felt sure would be there, and inwardly appalled at her panic-stricken outburst.

The silence between them lengthened, and when at last she looked at him she found the bright blue gaze fixed on her with an oddly gentle regard. He shook his head reprovingly.

"Haven't I told you before about going around in clothes that aren't warm enough?" he asked mildly. "It's freezing outside, didn't you think to wear a coat?"

She stared at him. Quite obviously he suffered from some weird obsession about catching cold, so much so that he hadn't taken in what she had just said. "I'm not concerned about putting on my coat," she retorted. "I've just handed in my resignation, and that seems more important to me than whether I'm warm enough or not."

"Yes. Yes, of course." His tone was that of someone humouring a fractious child, and Coralie felt the hot colour rush to her cheeks. In all her life she had never met anyone who could so easily put her at a disadvantage.

"Now," he said, "tell me exactly what's troubling you."

"But I've just told you," she said plaintively. "I've had second thoughts about the job. It's bigger than I thought—with more responsibility. I'm—I'm frightened of letting you down!"

At once two big hands took hold of hers. She raised startled amber eyes to his, and at the same moment something moved in the deep recesses of her heart, as if an untried bell had swung of its own accord to toll a first, echoing note. The sensation was gone in an instant, but as the firelight flickered on Scarlett's dark features, and the warm hands enclosed hers, Coralie felt tension drain from her and tranquility take its place.

"I knew at once it was a mistake to have told you how much we're putting into the project," he said. "From that moment you've been a bundle of nerves. I realise it may sound a lot of money to you, but it's by no means an unusual amount to invest in a scheme of this size. More important is your loss of confidence in yourself."

Speechless, she nodded, and waited for him to continue.

"Why do you think I chose you out of a hundred and fifty applicants?" he asked calmly.

"A hundred and—? But—I thought there were fifteen?"

"So there were—at the Dorchester, but only one in ten of those who applied were called for interview. I liked your design at first sight, and I liked it even more made up. Also I liked the selection of drawings you brought to the interview, and the fact that you hadn't tried to impress with way-out ideas, but had thought about your basic materials. Add to that your sound training in design, your fresh uninhibited eye for line and colour, and a certain, quite unmistakable flair, and you'll perhaps see that the decision wasn't too difficult. I give you my solemn promise that you won't be asked to do more than you're capable of."

Such was the power of his personality, the reassurance he conveyed, that like one hypnotised Coralie found herself nodding, smiling, and eventually apologising. She edged her hands from his grasp. "I'm sorry, Mr. Scarlett. When I saw how huge the mill is and—and everything, I'm afraid I—well, I panicked, that's all I can say."

"All the best artists suffer from stage-fright," he said comfortingly. "And you can come to me if things get too much for you."

It was kind of him to say that, she told herself. But it struck her as most unfitting that a new employee should go running to the Managing Director every time she had some little worry on her mind, like a child to the teacher in nursery school. She gathered a few remnants of self-possession around her and jumped to her feet, anxious to get out before she made herself look more of a fool than she had done already.

"One more thing, before you dash off," said Scarlett, moving towards her quickly. But before he could continue, the study door opened and a woman came in, stopping just inside the doorway and looking with some surprise at Coralie who was standing there with Scarlett's detaining hand on her arm.

The newcomer advanced with what Coralie at once recognised as the practised glide of the professional model. "Hello, darling," she said huskily, proffering a smooth, tinted cheek for Scarlett to kiss. "Sorry to butt in, but the front door wasn't locked, and you said you'd probably be working until I arrived."

"You know I've told you to come straight in when you call," he said easily. "Meet Coralie Dee, our new designer—you remember I was telling you about her."

A burning desire to know exactly what it was he had "told about her" immediately overcame Coralie, so that she almost missed the name when Scarlett introduced the new arrival. "Coralie, this is Janice Ellison, a friend of mine, who has half-promised to do some of the modelling for the catalogue."

He was a high-flyer, Coralie thought admiringly, looking with interest at the other woman. She had seen that lovely face in many a top-flight fashion magazine. The luminous green eyes and fine-boned features were highly photogenic, and just different enough from the currently fashionable look to attract attention. But it wasn't the eyes which captivated her so much as the dark, beautifully-cut hair, which swung smoothly just below the ears. It was so incredibly glossy that she could hardly stop staring at it, thinking how different it was from the shaggy frizz of many present-day models.

She smiled at the older woman as they shook hands. "I've seen lots of your photographs, Miss Ellison," she said warmly. "I'm sure if you model items from the new collection it will be a marvellous boost to sales."

Janice Ellison responded with a surprisingly impish grin, which sat oddly on the dramatically lovely face. "I'm thinking about it very seriously," she admitted. As she spoke she slid out of her honey-coloured fur coat, and Coralie recognised it as the one worn by Scarlett's companion when she had watched them enter the house in the early hours of the morning.

The older woman let Scarlett take the coat, revealing a simply cut dress in fine jade-green wool, with a single heavy chain of silver around her neck. With her colouring and streamlined figure the effect was stunning, so that Coralie could cheerfully have sunk through the floor in her old tie-and-dye caftan. What on earth had possessed her to come running across looking such a freak—and with her hair secured in its plait by, of all things, a piece of string?

Hurriedly she made her excuses, and Scarlett accompanied her to the door, but before opening it he took an overcoat from the closet and helped her into it, not speaking meanwhile, as if words were unnecessary for such a sensible procedure.

"You can let me have it back any time," he said as she left. "And I usually leave for the mill at eight-thirty, so if you're ready by then I'll take you down with me."

It seemed pointless and rather ungracious to protest. After all, he had been remarkably decent when his new employee attempted to resign before she had even officially started work.

She looked up at him and said seriously, "Thank you for being so—so nice, Mr. Scarlett."

He smiled then. That rare, brilliantly attractive smile which seemed positively to glitter with suppressed vitality. "I've been called many things in my time," he replied in amusement, "but 'nice' isn't the adjective most commonly used, I assure you. When you know me better you probably won't use it, either. See you tomorrow."

From the engulfing depths of his overcoat she smiled back at him, then hurried away to the coach-house, her confidence restored; and only the memory of how awful she had looked in comparison to the elegant Janice prevented the return of her usual sunny optimism. She placed the coat carefully on a hanger, and for an instant laid her cheek against the thick cloth, asking herself rather aggressively why on earth she shouldn't, when she liked the feel of it against her skin and the faintly heathery smell of the tweed.

Later, in the moment between waking and sleeping, she reflected that if Jethro Scarlett had been a less persuasive man she would probably be out of a job at this very moment, and faced with the prospect of returning home to explain to Francine and all her friends that she had been too scared even to make a start. She should be falling on his neck in gratitude, really she should.

But the thought came to her, slowly and insidiously, that whatever the outcome, Scarlett had handled her with remarkable skill. Using only two or three sentences and a warm handclasp he had made her change her mind with something of the expertise of a puppeteer manipulating his doll.

It wasn't a pleasant thought. In fact it was positively painful to a spirited and independent girl like Coralie. And as for falling on his neck in gratitude—it seemed highly probable that anything of that sort, whether out of gratitude or for a more intimate reason, would be the province of Janice Ellison, and certainly not that of his most recent employee.

It gave Coralie intense pleasure next morning to walk into her studio at the mill in the knowledge that this was her own domain where, with a lot of hard work and some inspiration, she could create a set of designs which would either put her on the road to a successful career or plunge her back into total obscurity.

The room was on the top floor, light and airy, and partitioned out of what had originally been the completely open floor of the spinning-room. Since those early days every process of manufacture had been revised and mechanised, and now the fourth floor was taken up by offices, laboratories, and experimental workshops, and a lift hummed smoothly up and down next to the square corner tower which housed the great stone staircase.

Scarlett had left her at the studio door with a nod of his dark head and a brisk "See you later." She had been relieved when he made no mention of what had happened between them the previous evening. If anything, he had seemed at pains to treat her as just another employee, an attitude which suited her very well.

She slipped into one of the pretty working smocks that Francine had made for her in the few hectic days before she left home. It was in sunshine yellow cotton, gathered from a frilled yoke, with two patch pockets made in the form of big white daisies, and it had the effect of making her feel ready for work but at the same time colourful and, somehow, a trifle high-spirited.

For a few minutes she wandered about the room, examining the equipment more closely than she had liked to do when Scarlett had shown her round the previous day. Bolts of cloth and thick wads of samples were stacked against one wall. A group of dressmaker's dummies stood in the corner, grotesquely headless and legless as they waited to be clothed. A wide, heavy work-bench ran the full length of the window wall, and nearby was her easel, her drawing board, and all her drawing and painting materials. A small room leading off the studio was where her assistant would work, and this was equipped with sewing machines, steam presses, and everything she could possibly require for producing one-off models.

She had been both relieved and apprehensive when Scarlett told her that of course she would have someone to sew for her. A young woman with excellent qualifications had been brought in from a firm of ready-to-wear manufacturers in Leeds; a convenient arrangement all round as the girl in question was shortly to marry one of the lab technicians, himself a Raxby man.

Coralie had been relieved to know that she would have professional help in making up her originals, of course, but she couldn't help feeling apprehensive about whether she and her assistant would get on well together.

"How old is the girl who will be working with me?" she had asked Scarlett tentatively as they had walked the huge, echoing floors of the mill the day before. "I mean—will I have authority to tell her what to do?"

"Of course you will," he replied, and she could see again the quick, impatient toss of his head. "You are in charge of design for the ready-to-wear. She knows this, and will be under your orders. There'll be no problem there."

Uneasily she awaited the arrival of her assistant, and promptly at nine an earnest young man from Personnel brought her up to the studio, and after a few words of introduction left the two of them together.

The girl from Leeds was a curvaceous little red-head, not unlike the one Coralie had met so briefly at the Dorchester. "Everyone calls me Liz," she announced. "I was thrilled when Mr. Scarlett asked me to come here, because it means I'll be able to work on our cottage with Rob, instead of being miles away in Leeds until the wedding."

It was obvious she favoured the direct approach. In two minutes it was settled that she would address Coralie as such, and not Miss Dee or any nonsense of that kind, and that the little machine-room would be her own small province, leaving the big studio for Coralie. Two more minutes and Coralie knew that Liz was twenty-four, that her fiancé was Rob Bradley, that at first they would be living in a rented stone-built cottage owned by Scarlett, that Liz planned to carry on working for three years, by which time she and Rob would be buying a modern house of their own and she would, she hoped, be expecting her first baby.

Coralie was slightly overcome by such directness, and doubted whether she would be able to tell so downright a person what or what not to do. But she needn't have worried. Liz sat herself at her machine, rolled up her sleeves and looked at Coralie expectantly. "Fire away," she said easily. "You're the boss. I've had it in no uncertain terms from J.J. himself that I'm working for you!"

And that was the beginning of a friendship which was to support and sustain Coralie through the months of sheer hard work, which at times were to prove exhausting, at other times frustrating, but never for one single moment were they to prove dull.

Scarlett whirled in later in the morning, finding them both experimenting with pocket detailing on a loose-woven tweed. After a polite greeting, Liz disappeared to her room to continue sewing, and with a quick movement of his head towards the door, Scarlett asked quietly, "All right?"

Coralie smiled. Relief at working so well with Liz and the sheer easing of tension now that she was getting on with the job made her forget all about the little formal barriers which she had intended to erect between this disturbing man and herself. She had no idea of the radiance of her smile as she answered him.

"Oh yes. She's a treasure. A good worker, very capable, and extremely well briefed in advance. Thanks."

The blue eyes flickered over her, taking in the long silky blonde hair and the bright yellow smock. For a moment he hesitated, his eyes searching her face absently, as if the words he had intended speaking were suddenly lost to him. Then he shook his head slightly and carried on. "The working committee want a preliminary discussion about the project at 2:30. Timing, publication dates, sizings, maybe even a pooling of ideas about the catalogue lay-out. But most important of all at this stage, a clarification of exactly who we're aiming at. Just a few of us—our marketing man, P.R., advertising, productions manager, and a few more. My office. Can you make it?"

She was being tossed in at the deep end with a vengeance, but there would be no more panicking, on that she was determined.

Calmly she said, "Of course, Mr. Scarlett. I'll look forward to it," and with that reached for her pad of cloth samples and selected another one.

But Scarlett didn't leave at once. He leaned forward with his hands flat on the work-bench looking out of the big window. Outside on the great curving shoulder of the moor a weather-worn outcrop of rock stood darkly against the sky, and he stared as if deep in thought at the remains of a snow-drift lying at its base.

"My secretary tells me you brought very little baggage with you," he remarked. "Have you made arrangements for the rest to be sent on? If so, one of the works vans can pick it up for you. I intended asking you last night, but we were interrupted."

Coralie almost ground her teeth. Was she to be compelled for evermore to keep on explaining that she was not well-endowed with this world's goods? And had Miss Silverwood nothing better to do than provide inventories of her meagre belongings? But he was trying to be helpful. Give him credit for that.

"I'm sorry to labour the point yet again," she said gently, "but I really haven't an enormous amount of stuff to bring up here. The only things I left behind were a few favourite records and a very old record-player. I hope, now that I'm earning more, to buy a better one, and maybe replenish my wardrobe." Some perverse impulse made her add, a trifle acidly, "I might even replace that 'rubbishy coat' before long."

The dark-lashed eyelids came down, effectively concealing his reaction to that. "Mm," he said coolly. "And a good thing, too. See you at 2:30."

As soon as the door closed behind him Liz reappeared. "He's a dish, isn't he?" she asked in the practical tone of one comparing prices at the supermarket.

"What? Oh—yes. Yes, I suppose he is." In truth there was no other answer she could give. The human dynamo could, she supposed, be described as a dish. Among other things, she added silently.

Liz chuckled. "Rob says all the girls in the mill are crazy about him, but he never goes for the locals. He always picks gorgeous birds from further afield."

There was no hint of malice in the remark, just a straight statement of fact as she had heard it. But Coralie felt oddly reluctant to start discussing Scarlett, even though she was extremely curious about him.

"Try reinforcing these pocket flaps a little more strongly, will you Liz?" she asked, and at once her companion shot off to oblige. Thoughtfully Coralie turned back to the bench.

Snowflakes were whirling on the wind when she left the mill just before six. Liz had departed promptly at five, explaining in her customary forthright manner that she would work like mad during her set hours, but after that—no chance! Rob, she said, finished at the same time and would be waiting to run her back to her auntie's house, where she was living until the wedding.

It occurred to Coralie that everyone hereabouts was related to someone else. Even the production manager and the P.R. man were brothers. Only Scarlett himself appeared to be bereft of family; although Raxby could be teeming with his relations for all she knew, of course.

She held on to her hood as she crossed the road to the phone box. The conference in Scarlett's office had been immensely interesting, and she felt that as a complete newcomer she had not acquitted herself too badly; in fact a few of her more daring suggestions had met with almost embarrassing approval.

Francine must have been hovering near the phone because she lifted the receiver at the first ring, and listened in evident relief to Coralie's account of her first day. "And what do you think, *Maman*? It's snowing!"

Francine exclaimed in surprise, and then laughed. "That will suit you, *chérie*. But how strange to have snow—it has been a lovely spring day down here."

When their goodbyes were said Coralie went out into the dancing white flakes with almost childish pleasure. It rarely snowed at home, although heavy falls on nearby Exmoor were not uncommon.

She thought, as she climbed the hill, that during

45

the evening she would work on the collar detail of the tweed coat, and maybe watch television for a while. Then, in the morning, if everywhere was covered in snow, she would set off before J.J. Scarlett could give her a lift, and tramp down to the mill on her own, enjoying every minute of it.

Lost in a maze of happy and rather confused thoughts about the job, her flat, the snow, and the untold advantages of working in North Yorkshire, she reached the courtyard and made for her staircase, where each step was already padded with white.

Scarlett's car stopped in front of the garage as she climbed. He tooted the horn in greeting and she waved and went on climbing, uncertain whether she was pleased or sorry to have missed his company on the journey home.

She switched on the outside light and was unlocking the door when he spoke right behind her. The sound of his footsteps on the stairs had been muffled by the snow and she almost shot out of her skin when the deep voice said, "Coralie—I'm sorry. I didn't mean to startle you. I just wanted to say that as far as I'm concerned your first day has been a great success."

"Oh—thank you." That was nice to know, anyway.

"But you don't need to stay so late, you know, just because you have no set times to start and finish. You mustn't feel compelled to put in the sort of hours I do."

"I stayed a little later because I wanted to make a phone call on the way back," she explained, seeking to emphasise that she had no intention of using the phone at the house.

"Goodnight, Mr. Scarlett. And—please don't bother to give me a lift tomorrow. I'll walk down when I'm ready."

He looked at the snow-petalled circle of light spilling from the little landing. "Oh no," he said flatly. "No. The snow has set in, I'm afraid."

She beamed at him. "Yes. Isn't it lovely? I shall walk down tomorrow and really enjoy it."

He sighed audibly, and to her astonishment pushed her none too gently inside and ran an irate hand through his snow-dusted hair. "Let's get this quite clear," he said decisively. "The snow up here is not for little kiddie-winkies to make pretty snowmen. These hills are dangerous, doubly so in bad weather. Even in broad daylight they are hazardous when it snows, and under no circumstances can I have you wandering about them."

Coralie's full lips jutted out ominously. "But I shan't be wandering. I shall only go down to the mill. And I'll wear my boots . . ."

"If the snow is more than an inch or two deep you will go down with me," he said coolly. "I have a Land-Rover for bad weather, and if it's too deep to use that, you will stay up here. Is that clear?"

For the first time in their brief acquaintance she saw all too clearly the ruthlessness which lay beneath the dynamic charm. This was the real man, the man who ran the business empire of Scarlett's.

"Is that clear?" he repeated.

"Yes. It's clear," she admitted, a trifle sulkily.

"Right!" He turned and went down the stairs.

She slammed the door so hard in temper that it shook at the hinges. A fat chance there was of being able to live independently and without interference when she was within reach of him!

Such was the turmoil of her thoughts that she had been indoors for half an hour before she noticed the hi-fi system. Sleek and gleaming and obviously expensive, it was wired up on either side of the fireplace. Was she seeing things? Surely it hadn't been there before?

Hesitantly she examined it. A note lay on top of one of the speakers, hand-written in a firm, legible hand.

This hi-fi is one which I seldom use. Perhaps you would care to borrow it until you buy one of your own? Also, please accept the loan of a few records, on the off-chance that one or two may appeal to you.

J.J.S.

Coralie sank down on the rug as if felled by a blow, her pleasure tinged with bewilderment. She would never make him out. Never. One minute he was horrible, the next he made some gesture like this which was totally unexpected and incredibly thoughtful. Even his note was so tactfully worded as to make it easy for her to accept without sacrificing her pride.

But of course! She mustn't forget his big plan to keep her happy; it was all part and parcel of that. Hadn't he said he knew creative people must be kept happy in order to "deliver the goods"?

Yes, that was it. Keep the temperamental little thing content at all costs, even if it meant phoning the house and dashing back up here during the day and writing notes and selecting records. With a cynicism which would have astounded her mother, Coralie flipped through the thirty or so records which were there. Pop, traditional jazz, several light classics and a selection of more serious stuff right through to a couple of Mahler symphonies and a recent recording of Stockhausen. Oh yes, it would be easy to find something she liked amongst all those.

Without hesitation she selected the first symphony of Sibelius, a great favourite of hers. Not until the familiar opening notes sounded through the steeply raftered room did she recall that it had been this very symphony which Scarlett had been playing in the seclusion of his study when she descended on him the previous evening.

Thoughtfully she reached for her sketching block, and started to draft different versions of collars for the tweed coat. Had he sent across one of his own personal favourites? If so, it seemed that they had one thing in common, at least.

Four

The snow stayed for the rest of the week, until on Sunday it disappeared in a quick thaw beneath heavy rain. Coralie had accompanied Scarlett in the Land-Rover each day with every appearance of docility, and then spent her lunch-hours going for long walks in the fields behind the mill, until even she had to admit that her high-heeled boots weren't up to it.

Liz had been intrigued to learn that Scarlett drove Coralie to and from work. "Good grief!" she exclaimed, eyeing her speculatively. "To think of the great J.J. himself ferrying you around like that! Do you think he fancies you?"

"Of course not," said Coralie shortly. "It's because I live almost on his door-step, and he regards the cold and the snow as sworn enemies."

Liz was silent for a moment, then she said: "I'm not surprised. Wasn't there something a long time ago about his girl-friend dying of exposure up on the moors?"

"Dying? On the moors?" For a moment Coralie struggled against nausea, and closed her eyes quickly, recalling how she had inwardly mocked his concern about her catching cold and going out in the snow.

"Yes," Liz was saying. "I'm sure my auntie told me about it once. But it all happened years ago, when he was young."

"He isn't exactly ancient now," pointed out Coralie.

"No, I know. But this was when he was only about twenty, I think. I'll ask auntie, she'll remember."

"Don't bother—thanks all the same. I'd rather not know." Her vivid imagination had already set the scene.

Liz looked at Coralie, her puggy little face concerned and rather surprised. "You're as pale as a ghost," she chided. "You mustn't get all upset. It happened ages ago. And another thing—all this wandering about in the snow every lunch-hour hasn't done you any good at all; neither has working till after six each evening until his Lordship condescends to take you home. You look tired!"

It was strange that Liz should have used the same phrase as Scarlett—"wandering about." It conjured up visions of someone half-demented. In spite of herself Coralie giggled.

"That's better," said Liz immediately. "See you on Monday. Don't eat too many cakes at Sunday tea!"

The last remark was a reference to Coralie's invitation from Miss Silverwood. The secretary had come round to the studio one afternoon, and in her own very pleasant and unassuming way had asked Coralie to visit her.

Not even to herself would Coralie have admitted that she had sometimes felt just the tiniest bit lonely up in her flat when the wind howled across the hills and the snow lay in pleated drifts over the moors. And so she accepted the invitation warmly, quelling the suspicion that Miss Silverwood was acting on Scarlett's instructions as part of his "keep Coralie happy" campaign.

Now she was ready to set off, having taken some trouble with her appearance; wearing her only decent dress, a tight-waisted, full skirted creation of her own in dark green corduroy, and with her hair swathed into a figure-of-eight chignon.

Standing at the big window she looked out across

the wet fields, debating whether to get a soaking or to ask Mrs. Braithwaite for the loan of an umbrella. Then the doorbell rang.

It was Scarlett, standing there in the pouring rain with his shirt sticking damply to his chest. Apparently he didn't always follow his own advice about dressing according to the weather.

"Come in," she said, hurriedly making way for him.

"Sylvie—Miss Silverwood—has just been on the phone to say don't set out in the rain, she'll come and pick you up. But as I'm going that way myself I said I'd drop you off. Do you want to go now, or later?"

Helplessly she looked up at him. It seemed she was fated to be constantly carted around in this man's cars. "It's very kind of you both. I'll go whenever you're ready."

She saw him look across at the designs spread over the dining-table, and waited for some reaction, but he made no comment. "I'll be ready in five minutes," he said, and departed.

For reasons best known to himself he had wasted few words on her since the exchange between them at the top of the staircase in the snow. Even when she had thanked him earnestly for the loan of the hi-fi, his reaction had not exactly encouraged pleasant conversation.

"For goodness' sake stop falling over yourself thanking me every time we meet," he said irritably. "It's not necessary. And by the way, I've arranged for you to have an advance on your salary in case you need it, so don't thank me for that, either. It will be stopped out of your money at the end of the month."

His attitude throughout the week had been brisk and business-like, but it disconcerted her to find that by the end of the week she hurried to answer the studio phone in expectation of hearing the deep, decisive tones. Not only that, each time the studio door opened and someone else came in, she knew the oddest and most ridiculous sense of dis-appointment.

Still, she told herself philosophically, if she chose to work for a human dynamo, it was only to be expected that she would feel some sort of reaction to the current he generated.

She already knew a little about the geography of Raxby, and as they swished along towards Miss Silverwood's house she said curiously, "I thought this road petered out very soon? Doesn't it turn into a single track leading to Raxby High Moor?"

He nodded. "One reason for the valley being so unspoilt is that there is no through road, merely a few tracks over the top," explained Scarlett. "But in case your pride is outraged and you think I've come this way specially to drop you off, let me set your mind at rest. I'm on my way to visit friends up on Raxby High."

Well, she had deduced he was visiting someone, she told herself, having seen a sheaf of red roses in the back of the car when she took her place next to him.

"The flowers are lovely, aren't they?" she asked as he stopped the car outside a stone-built house set against the hillside.

He leaned across the front of her to open the door, and she caught the scent of his skin, clean and fresh, and as he turned his head she looked into the vivid blue eyes at closer quarters than she had seen them before. At once, clearer and more insistent than the first time, it seemed that the great bell swung and tolled in her heart, becoming one with her heart-beat and causing her chest to tighten in an effort to steady her breathing.

He answered her question with a perfectly straight face. "I prefer primroses," he said.

She got out of the car, colour rising in her cheeks as the implication of his words hit her. Then, with a casual lift of his hand and a nod of the dark head he drove away, heading for the moors.

Sunday tea at Miss Silverwood's was a substantial meal, Coralie found, as she tucked into cold ham and salad with hot potato fritters, followed by trifle and three kinds of cake. "That was delicious," she said at last. "No, I couldn't eat another crumb. In fact, I shall soon have to watch my weight, because I'm constantly hungry since coming to live up here."

"It's the air," said Miss Silverwood. "It always affects newcomers like that, especially if they're from milder areas. It makes you feel wide awake, doesn't it?"

Coralie smiled. "Just as well, with the human dynamo around." She stopped, rather embarrassed at using that name to describe Scarlett, but Miss Silverwood threw back her head and laughed heartily.

"So that's what you call him! Very apt! Mind you it's a good thing he *is* a human dynamo, because ten years ago the firm was in a bad way, and it's mainly due to his energy and hard work that it's thriving today. Raxby would have been a sorry place if the mill had closed."

"Are there no other members of the family to help him run things?"

"Not really. He has a sister, but she is away over the hills in the Lake District, married to a farmer, and with two little girls. Jethro was the older of two brothers, you know, but many years ago the younger one, Ralph, was killed in a car crash. The shock of it almost killed his father, as well, and for a long time he was a semi-invalid, until he died last year. Jethro was hardly out of university before he took over the reins and became Managing Director. Now he is Chairman of the Board as well, and the best I've ever seen."

"And his mother?" asked Coralie gently.

"Oh, she was a pretty little soul who died when the children were all small."

Coralie was silent, her thoughts not on Scarlett's pretty little mother, but on a young girl found dead out on the snow-covered hills, and she knew with swift insight that whatever happened she could never bring herself to question anyone about it.

"Mr. Scarlett certainly seems to work very hard," she ventured, dragging her thoughts back to their conversation. "Does he play hard as well?" It was a rather idiotic question, but the older woman seemed to see nothing odd about it.

"Oh, yes. He's always off to some party or other, and he always has plenty of female company. But I wish he would fall in love with some nice girl—someone he wanted to marry and who would make him happy."

It was no use, Coralie couldn't resist the temptation to ask, "What about Miss Ellison? They seem fond of each other."

Shrewd grey eyes looked into hers. "Oh, you've met, have you? She's nice enough in her way, I suppose, and she lives nearer than most of the others, but she isn't the one I would choose for him."

If Janice Ellison lived nearby it was more than likely that she was the friend he was visiting on Raxby High Moor. Not that she was surprised at that. Coralie was intrigued by the almost motherly air of concern shown by Scarlett's secretary. But that lady was not disposed to chat about her employer any longer, and with gentle good humour she changed the subject.

It proved to be an enjoyable evening. Coralie got on well with the older woman, and before she drove her home Miss Silverwood showed her over the house. "It's lovely," said Coralie sincerely, "so beautifully decorated—and your furniture is marvellous."

"Most of it has come down from the family," said the other. "It's mid-Victorian, and as I'm interested in sales I've picked up a few bits and pieces of my own here and there. Have you seen Mr. Scarlett's furniture at all? He has some lovely stuff, but much earlier than mine."

"No, not really. I've just seen the hall and the

inside of his study, and that only briefly. I also have his permission to use the studio if I like."

"Oh yes. Judith—you know—Mrs. Braithwaite, was telling me about that. I think she will be pleased if the room is used more often. Mr. Scarlett hasn't really got the time these days, and Adrian has left us, so it's used very little."

"Was Adrian the textile designer who had my flat?"

"Yes. He expected to be given the job you've now got—even though he wasn't really qualified. Mr. Scarlett wouldn't let him have it, so he went off to work for one of our competitors."

"Oh." There wasn't much else to say, really, thought Coralie.

Later, preparing for bed, she felt a fleeting sympathy for the unknown Adrian. Had he really imagined he could battle against Scarlett's and win?

She awoke suddenly, hours later, and heard the soft swish of tyres on the drive. A car door closed quietly, but there was no sound of the car being garaged beneath her. She looked at the clock. Perhaps Scarlett was wary of disturbing her by putting the car away. After all, it was three o'clock in the morning.

Minutes later Coralie rearranged her pillows and snuggled down in bed. They certainly kept late hours up on Raxby High.

The next few days were busy, as usual, with the friendship between Coralie and Liz developing steadily. The fact that her wedding was only ten days distant had no effect on Liz's concentration. She still worked like a beaver.

"I suppose Leeds is too far for you to come to watch the wedding?" she asked Coralie rather wistfully one day. "Or are you going home for Easter?"

"No. It's such a distance to Somerset, and I've been here such a short time. I shall have a break from work, of course, and maybe explore the district a little."

"I'd ask you to come as a guest, but we're working to a tight budget, and we've invited everyone weeks ago," went on Liz with her usual frankness. "I'm not saying it will be the wedding of the year, but I would like you to see it."

"Of course I'll come," said Coralie warmly.

"I'll write it all out for you," promised the older girl, wrinkling her little snub nose affectionately. "Rob will be really pleased when I tell him you'll be there."

Coralie decided to take a walk round the mill, something which she often found helpful when thinking of a new design. She liked the mill, enjoying the noise, the bustle, the activity of it all, and already she was a familiar visitor in the weaving shed.

It was still called a "shed" although it was in fact a solid, modern building attached to the mill. Coralie loved to watch the cloth rolling from the looms, and she found that some of her best ideas were conceived amid the appalling noise and clatter.

"Good morning, Jim," she called to a grey-haired man setting up a loom with pale, misty-blue yarns. "Can I watch for a minute?"

The overlooker smiled across at her. "You won't disturb me, love," he shouted. "I can do this with my eyes shut!"

I expect you could, at that, thought Coralie, watching him closely. Absently she flicked back her hair as a loose blue thread descended on it.

Then Jim straightened up and smiled at someone behind her. "Mornin', Mr. Scarlett."

"Morning, Jim." The deep voice was wiped out as Jim switched on the loom, and Coralie turned to greet Scarlett. He looked livid with rage.

"Come with me," he bellowed, above the din, and to her amazement grasped her arm in a painful grip and hustled her from the shed.

It seemed very quiet in the covered passage which led to the mill, and her voice sounded too loud when she said shakily, "What—what's the matter?"

"Are you quite mad?" asked Scarlett furiously, facing her.

Coralie's temper rose to match his. "What are you talking about? You told me I could go anywhere in the mill, didn't you? It helps me when I see the cloth being woven."

"It wouldn't help you very much to be scalped, would it?" he asked cuttingly, and with one big hand he lifted the long hair from her shoulders. "Haven't you noticed that all the women, and for that matter any long-haired men, are wearing protective headgear?"

A nasty feeling of humiliation hit Coralie. What an idiot she was! Of course she should have known the dangers of long hair floating around near so much machinery.

"Why on earth Jim didn't tell you I don't know," Scarlett was muttering angrily, half turning.

"Oh please—don't mention it to him! You can't blame him for not telling me something I should have known already!" In her agitation she grasped his wrist as if to prevent him returning to tackle the amiable Jim. His skin felt cold and slightly rough, and as she hastily released him her fingers brushed the dark hairs on the back of his wrist.

Because she felt embarrassed by his outburst and furious with herself for blushing and babbling like a fool she dismissed the apology which had been half-formed in her mind. "I don't see that you needed to manhandle me in that offensive fashion!" she told him coldly.

"I once had to manhandle a woman who had half her head torn off," he retorted, "it was not a pleasant experience. But I'm sorry if I upset you by grabbing you. Unexpected physical contact can be very upsetting, can't it?" Deliberately he looked at his wrist, as if expecting to find the imprint of her fingers.

"Oh!" Words failed her. He was impossible! Turning away from him she marched rapidly along the passage, leaving him standing by the doors of the weaving shed.

Once inside the mill itself she ignored the lift and started up the wide stone stairs, dashing up them at top speed in an effort to work off her temper.

At the third floor she slowed down a little. He was a perfect horror, but he was right. Impatiently she hurried up the next flight and rushed into the studio. Grabbing a comb from her bag she tidied her hair and plaited it out of the way, tying the end with an off-cut of cloth.

"What's all that for?" asked Liz curiously.

"I've just been told off for having my hair loose in the mill. J.J. saw me near a loom in the weaving shed."

Liz whistled through pursed lips. "Sorry love. I let you in for that. I told him you were likely to be there. He came in here looking for you."

Coralie stared. "What did he want, did he say?"

"No, he just went out like a whirlwind, as he usually does. You'd better ring him and find out, hadn't you?"

"Certainly not," declared Coralie haughtily. "If he wants something, let him ring me!"

Liz went quietly back to her machine with the air of one humouring a lunatic.

A moment later the phone rang. It was Scarlett. "Do you think you could stay put long enough for me to ask you something?" he asked politely.

"Yes, of course." Her voice was expressionless.

"I've had a long chat with Greenfield's in Leeds— the firm we're hoping will agree to do the making-up. Roger Greenfield wants to come over this afternoon, and is keen to meet you. Are you free?"

"Of course I am, if you want me to be." Honestly, all this elaborate courtesy when he knew perfectly well she would have to be free if he said so!

"Right. Come along at 2:30, will you? Then you

can both go off and mull over the designs. He wants to be sure you realise that too much intricate detail will affect his costs."

"But we've been into all that, Mr. Scarlett. You know I'm keeping production costs in mind all the time."

"Yes, I know that, but he doesn't, and I think he wants to see for himself what you've come up with so far. He strikes a hard bargain, does Greenfield, and I'd be pleased if you'd humour him over this."

Coralie thought rapidly for a moment. "I see. I'll come to your office at 2.30 then, Mr. Scarlett. Yes. Thank you. Goodbye."

She went to tell Liz. "Roger Greenfield is coming over this afternoon. Was he your boss back in Leeds?"

"He's the son of the boss, actually, but he's taking charge more and more as his father gets nearer retiring age. He's a bit of a whizz-kid is our Mr. Roger. Very sharp, very bright, almost as good as he thinks he is."

Coralie's heart sunk at that. Not another human dynamo to contend with, surely? "What is he like?"

"Loaded with charm. But not good-looking; not a dish like J.J. Will you go to meet him in your overall? And with your hair tied up with that bit of old tweed?"

"Why not?" asked Coralie, still feeling on edge. "He's coming to see the designs, isn't he, not me?"

"Oh, of course, it's up to you," agreed Liz hurriedly. "I just thought it would smooth the way for future involvement with him if you get off to a good start, that's all."

"I have no intention of getting dolled up just to keep on the right side of Roger Greenfield," began Coralie. Then she looked down at Liz's concerned, pudgy little face. She was talking sense, as usual. "But Liz, I'm not dressed to impress. You know I wear any old thing under my smocks!"

"Let's have a look," said Liz, practical as ever.

"Mm, that skirt is O.K.—I like the braid—but your sweater has seen better days, hasn't it? And those shoes! And what about your hair—would you like me to put it up or something?"

Promptly at 2:30 Coralie arrived at Scarlett's office. She was wearing strappy shoes belonging to Liz her own dark red braided skirt, and a black silky cardigan, also from Liz, worn the wrong way round so that it buttoned all the way up the back. Her hair was swathed smoothly into a gleaming coil behind her ears, and the general effect was very different from the long-haired girl in her pretty green smock.

Just for a second she thought she saw surprise in Scarlett's blue gaze, and then she was being introduced to Roger Greenfield. He was a stocky, thick-necked young man, beautifully dressed in a dark business suit. His hair was a mass of pale blond curls, growing low on his forehead and neck, but cropped close to his head, so that it had an odd resemblance to the curly white pelt on the head of a young Hereford bull. A broad flat nose increased the likeness, but when he smiled his beautiful even teeth transformed him back into an engaging young man.

He held her hand too long. She had met his kind before—often, but she soon saw that Liz had been right when she described him as a charmer. He was brash and more than a little cocky, but in seconds she felt at ease with him, more so than with Scarlett.

Her employer sat impassively behind his desk, saying a few words from time to time, but in the main leaving the talking to the other two.

Before long Roger suggested moving on to the studio. She remained helpful and friendly towards him, rather enjoying the way he put himself out to be agreeable. What a pleasant change after the bossy and dogmatic Scarlett.

"Well, we've cleared up several points that were troubling me, J.J." said Roger on leaving. "I'll give

61

you a ring tomorrow." With that he took Coralie firmly by the elbow and led her from the room.

In the studio he greeted Liz easily. "Hello, Liz. How's the prospective bride? Don't let us disturb you. I'm just going through the designs with Coralie."

Liz took the hint and went back to her sewing, while Coralie spread her completed drawings over the work bench, and brought out the models which had been made up so far.

The next half-hour was a strange blend of flirtation on his part and technical discussion between them both.

"You're pretty well up on our side of things," he said admiringly, at one stage. "Have you worked in the rag trade?"

"Yes, I did some practical training in industry during my design course, and I've worked in the trade during some of my vacations."

"That's a terrific help. No wonder you've got the hang of things from the manufacturing point of view." Then with barely a pause he added, "I'd like to take you out for the evening some time soon, Coralie. Purely pleasure—no business. Would you like that?"

She looked into the confident, light-blue eyes just level with her own. He was rather nice, after all; the brash, bull-like Greenfield Junior. And what relaxing company after Scarlett.

"I'd love to," she said honestly.

"Great! I'll give you a ring in the next day or two and we'll fix something up," he promised.

As soon as he had gone Liz appeared, grinning triumphantly. "I told you he was full of the old charm, didn't I? Not to mention loaded with sex-appeal. I couldn't help hearing him ask you out. Do you want to change sweaters again, or shall we stay as we are? I don't mind."

"Let's swap back now," said Coralie, anxious to relieve Liz of her old grey sweater and flat shoes. "I'm awfully grateful, Liz. And it's taught me not to wear horrible old clothes under my smocks. I'll be prepared in future. In fact, I might buy a few tops and things at the end of the month."

She was thinking about her budget as she hung up her smock at six-thirty that evening. Francine had decided to carry on working two days a week at the shop now that the winter was almost over, but at Coralie's insistence she had promised to cut down on her dressmaking for a few months at least.

But even after sending home a sizeable contribution Coralie reckoned she could still buy some good shoes and a couple of sweaters. Any sewing for herself would have to wait until she was less involved at work.

She was turning off the lights, still deep in thought, when the door opened and Scarlett stood silhouetted against the brightness of the corridor.

"Oh—" She wished he wouldn't appear so silently. That was the second time he had frightened the life out of her. The rest of the studio was already in darkness so she paused in the act of switching off the lights above the workbench, her arm still upraised. I hope he doesn't realise where the black cardigan must have come from, she thought suddenly, but she had forgotten that there was little he missed, and she saw the keen glance linger over her grey sweater and pass on.

"I was crossing the yard to go home when I saw your lights still on," he said. "Do you want a lift back?"

It was the first time he had offered since the snow went, and she could hardly refuse since he'd come all the way back to ask her. "Thank you. Yes."

Going down in the lift he was silent, but once in the car he said quietly. "Coralie, I think you're overdoing it a bit. Things are well up to date, why not finish a little earlier?"

"I enjoy it," she assured him. "I don't mind staying on to finish something if it's going well."

"As you wish. It's up to you," he said, the keen gaze leaving the road just for a moment and meeting hers. "I have no complaints about the staff at the mill, but I must admit I don't usually have actively to discourage someone from working. By the way, Judith has been on to me because I haven't asked you to dinner yet. She seems to think you might be existing on baked beans and boiled eggs."

Coralie laughed. "There's no fear of that! Your Yorkshire air has given me such an appetite I have a hot lunch in the canteen and then sometimes cook again in the evening. I'm always ravenous!"

"Good," he said, and left it at that.

He probably thinks that's let him off the hook, she thought, suddenly despondent.

Then he said: "Thanks for being so—obliging with Greenfield. But I've known Roger a long time, Coralie. I know how he operates. Don't think I expect you to be obliging outside working hours!" With a squeal of brakes he brought the car to an abrupt halt outside the garage.

She looked across at him with eyes that seemed huge in the darkness of the car. "Thank you, Mr. Scarlett. I appreciate that. But as a matter of fact he's already asked me out and I've accepted."

Scarlett stared straight ahead, his lean profile quite unreadable. "I see. Well, he always was a quick worker. I just wanted you to know how I felt about it, that's all."

There was a silence, an awkward silence, which Coralie finally ended by saying, rather quickly, "I'm sorry about this morning, Mr. Scarlett. It was stupid and thoughtless of me to go around with my hair flying all over the place."

His face was in shadow but she caught the gleam of his rare smile. "I'm sorry as well. I shouldn't have dragged you out of the weaving shed like that!"

For some strange reason Coralie's spirits soared immediately. There could have been no other excuse for saying so ridiculously: "Are we friends again?"

She thought she heard the faint breath of a sigh—and who could wonder at that, she asked herself, he must think he was dealing with a child. . . .

"Friends?" he asked slowly. "Yes, of course we are."

Then he leaned across and touched his lips to her cheek in a gentle little kiss.

It was a friendly, comforting gesture, nothing more, and there was no necessity at all to act as if she had been stung. She clapped one hand to her cheek and shot out of the car, making for the stairs at top speed, recalling just in time that she hadn't said goodbye.

She turned back to where he was still sitting in the driving seat, watching her.

"Goodnight, Mr. Scarlett," she said breathlessly. "Thanks for the lift." Then she went quickly up the stairs.

Five

The following week proved to be busier than ever in the studio, with Coralie and Liz trying to clear up all experimental sewing and also finish some original models before Liz went off for her wedding and honeymoon.

Coralie found herself working on designs in the evenings in order to spend her days sewing with Liz. She felt some relief when Roger Greenfield telephoned her to postpone their date. An outing with the cocky young clothing manufacturer would have made a welcome break from the pressure of work, but she could hardly spare the time.

The confident tones came over the line. "I've had to take over from our export manager who is away sick, so I shall be going on a round trip of the E.E.C. countries lasting about three weeks. I'll ring you as soon as I get back. By the way, I thought you'd like to know that I've just written to J.J. confirming that we will take on the making-up for the mail-order scheme, The contract is being drawn up today ready for when he gets back."

She was pleased at Roger's news about the contract. She liked him, even though he was pushy and so overpoweringly self-confident. It was a relief to know that the making-up of her designs would be under his capable direction.

She wondered what Scarlett would have to say about it on his return from Paris, although he would surely be pleased—he had been anxious enough for Greenfield's to take on the job.

Her mind drifted to what he might be doing at that moment, and she surrendered to an odd little bout of melancholy, something which had recurred at intervals ever since she learned that he was abroad. If she had not been so busy she would have tried to analyse her feelings about him, because they were by no means clear-cut; one moment she was furious with him, the next she was miserable because he was away.

It was all so at odds with her usual sunny temperament that it was almost a relief to be too busy to think about it, even if she had wanted to. And she wasn't sure that she did want to! She still cringed with embarrassment when she recalled their last meeting, and her childish query: "Are we friends again?"

The way he had sighed surely meant that his patience was being tried. As for that gentle little kiss—well, it was doubtless another of those thoughtful, rather touching little gestures, planned cold-bloodedly as part of his keep-her-happy campaign. She had received further proof of his efforts in that direction when Mrs. Braithwaite had called at the flat one evening with a newly-baked fruit cake. Over a cup of coffee Coralie had casually mentioned the way Scarlett had organised her arrival in Raxby at such short notice, and Judith had gone on to tell her of what had happened about her bedroom. It appeared that a furniture store in Leeds had received instructions to deliver new carpets, a bed and bed linen, and at top speed Walter had cleared out the more masculine furnishings in order to make way for the new items for Coralie.

It was another example of Scarlett's kindness and consideration—another example that he would go to any lengths to keep her happy so that she would "deliver the goods."

Feeling unaccountably tired-out and in low spirits Coralie swung the finished tweed coat on to the model for a last check, and looked at it with critical eyes. Yes, it had turned out well. Stylish, unusual, and with the stunningly beautiful cloth showing to full advantage.

She stuck her hands into the pockets of her smock and savoured the unique joy of the creative artist who looks at work that is good. A moment later, cheerful once more, she reached for her samples of dress-weight woollens and went in search of Liz.

"I've drawn you a plan of how to get to the church," announced the bride-to-be with enthusiasm. "It's not too far from the station, and you can get to the centre by bus afterwards if you want to do some shopping." She patted a parcel near her sewing machine. "And thanks again for the towels, Coralie, they're super."

The luxurious dark blue towels were Coralie's wedding present, ordered specially at the little draper's shop in the village after checking with the practical Liz that the colour was right. It had been a novel experience for Coralie to buy something without agonising over how much she could afford, and she had been grateful to Scarlett for arranging the advance on her salary.

Life as a designer certainly had its advantages, she thought as she balanced her budget that evening; she seemed to have an enormous amount of money now that she had been paid her first month's salary. She wrote a cheque to send off to her mother, then allocated living expenses for the coming month and earmarked something to save towards a new hi-fi. Even after that she was left with a sizeable sum. It was marvellous: she would buy something to wear. Perhaps she should forget about shoes and think about an evening dress. After all, if she went out with Roger she would have to look decent. According to Liz he liked his women well-turned-out, and that meant he would probably take her somewhere rather plush. Most of her previous dates had been with hard-up students, outings when the modest cost had been split fifty-fifty; it would be nice to sample the high-life for a change.

Then she tightened her lips, and even though she was alone the colour mounted to her cheeks. The man in her day-dream had somehow changed from Roger Greenfield to Scarlett, the human dynamo himself, generating his own unmistakable current. She would have to take herself in hand before she became obsessed by the man!

She watched television for a while, half her mind on the latest design, and when the news came on it barely registered with her until the word "Paris" was mentioned. A scheduled flight from Paris to Heathrow had crashed on take-off, with three passengers killed and several injured.

Her nerves jangling, Coralie sat motionless facing the screen. There was a silent session of question and answer going on in her head. It could be his plane. . . . Don't be an idiot, you don't even know when he's leaving Paris. . . . But surely he would be home for the Easter break? . . . Yes, but there are dozens of flights each day, how do you know this one is his? . . .

Of course, Mrs. Braithwaite would know! Quickly she ran down the steps and across the courtyard. The housekeeper answered her knock and didn't seem at all surprised to see her. "Oh, you've watched the news, have you? Yes, he was leaving Paris today but I don't know exactly when. He said he might stay in London for a few days before coming home."

"But business will be closed down for Easter," protested Coralie unthinkingly.

Mrs. Braithwaite looked intently at her flushed face. "I think perhaps he was intending to see—a friend," she explained gently.

Walter joined them then, his kind grey eyes concerned when he saw Coralie standing tensely by the door. "We've no way of knowing which flight he was on," he said. It was meant to be a sensible and comforting remark, but Coralie could see that both of them were deeply uneasy.

To her embarrassment she felt the sting of futile tears. "Can't you ring the airport? They have a list of passengers for each flight, don't they?"

Mrs. Braithwaite put a plump arm around her and led her to a kitchen chair. "Walter," she said over her shoulder, "put the kettle on." And to Coralie, "Come on, love, sit down. There's no need to get upset just yet."

With an effort Coralie pulled herself together before she became completely overwrought. She could hear Walter telephoning in the hall as Judith made a pot of tea.

"Aye, it was Mr. Scarlett's flight," he announced heavily from the kitchen door. "But he's all right. Very slightly injured, they said."

Judith sat down suddenly. "Well, he'll go to Miss Ellison's, I suppose. He'll be in touch as soon as he gets there, I expect. We'd better ring Bella, hadn't we? My sister Bella—Miss Silverwood," she explained to Coralie. "She can't have seen the news or she'd have been on the phone already."

Judith stood at the table ready to pour the tea. "And those other poor souls who were on the plane—they weren't all so lucky, were they?" Suddenly her plump features crumpled into tears of relief and reaction.

Coralie murmured something comforting and, the tea untouched, made her escape, leaving Walter patting Judith's shoulder helplessly.

Slowly she climbed the stairs to her flat. The wind had dropped, and large snowflakes spiralled down, patterning her sweater with white. She shivered as she reached the door; the last thing she could have borne was to stay chatting with Walter and Judith. She needed to be alone to savour the knowledge that Scarlett was safe.

For a few moments she abandoned herself to the heady sensation of relief which flowed through her, banishing the nightmare visions of that lean body maimed or even lifeless.

What did it matter that he was at Janice's flat, had perhaps intended to spend Easter there? He was safe. That was what mattered.

It was some time before she examined her own reactions to the accident. Had that really been her, babbling and crying? There could be only one reason for getting into such a state, and she was frightened to admit what it must be. She tried to analyse her feelings coolly and dispassionately, but her mind could only acknowledge that the bells in her heart were ringing out a positive carillon which raced joyously in time with her quickened heart-beat.

Bowing to the unmistakable, Coralie admitted to herself that she loved Jethro Scarlett. She lay back on the settee and stared up at the criss-crossed timbers of the roof, thinking back over their short but eventful acquaintance. That afternoon when she attempted to resign and he took hold of her hands—she had known then that something was happening to her. And looking back to her interview with him at the Dorchester she had to admit that from the first he had impressed her as no other man had ever done.

Dreamily she stared upwards, forgetting all the times he had made her furious, and for the present oblivious to the fact that he was probably in love with Janice.

Still in a happy daze she went to bed, and, worn out with the strain of the evening, fell at once into a deep, dreamless sleep.

The next morning she looked at the situation without her rose-tinted spectacles, and realised that if this was love it was not unmixed joy. It was pain, jealousy, uncertainty, and a quite overpowering yearning to see the man you loved. To be near

71

him, to hear him, to touch him. Well, perhaps the last was too much, she mustn't expect to touch him, but she longed with a desperate intensity to see him safe home, and if possible without the lovely Janice.

All right, so she was nurturing a love that had little hope of being returned, so she would settle for what was available to her. He liked her work, and even at times seemed to find her company enjoyable. That would do to be going on with.

In a sober frame of mind she decided to spend the day in the studio across at the house, even though it was Good Friday. It was warm and cosy, as it had been when she used it each evening while Scarlett was away. In case he arrived home unexpectedly she had dressed with care in her dark green dress and strappy shoes, with her freshly shampooed hair straight and shining about her shoulders.

In the middle of the morning Judith came in with coffee and a couple of freshly-baked hot cross buns. "Mr. Scarlett rang soon after you left last night," she informed Coralie. "He said he might stay in London for a day or two. Just as well really—his wrist is strapped up and it's a long drive back." As she went out she added casually, "I told him how upset you were last night."

Coralie stared after her. She hoped fervently that she had spared him the details. It was no part of her newly-formed plan to have Scarlett guess her feelings. She was going to be cool, friendly and efficient, and she was going to do all in her power to ensure that his mail-order scheme was a success. And that was all.

It was almost noon when the door opened. She looked up from her drawing board to see Scarlett in the doorway, standing next to the skein of faded red wool in its little glass case.

He looked pale and rather weary, with a lurid purple bruise crossing his cheekbone and running up into his hair. His left wrist was strapped up in some sort of bandage.

The colour ebbed from Coralie's face, leaving her cheeks feeling cold and waxy. She jumped from her stool and then, recollecting herself, stood still and forced a friendly smile to her lips.

"Hello, Mr. Scarlett. How are you?" As a greeting to the man she loved on his safe return, those few polite words would reveal nothing at all.

For a moment she thought he seemed perplexed, but perhaps she was mistaken, for he was looking at her with his usual cool, reflective expression as he stood in the doorway. "I'm all right, Coralie. Lucky to be alive, I suppose."

"Was it—awful?" She couldn't help asking the question, even though she knew it to be idiotic. An air crash was hardly likely to be enjoyable.

He gave the merest trace of a smile. "Yes," he agreed quietly, "it was awful. But it's good to be back."

Her spirits lifted at that. He was glad to be back! Unthinkingly she turned on him the full radiance of her smile. With no hint of a response he stared back at her sombrely. "What on earth are you doing working during the holiday?" he asked wearily. "Are you aiming to collapse from exhaustion?"

"Oh, for goodness' sake," she protested, at once discarding the cool, efficient image. "You must let me decide how much I'm capable of."

He eyed her face dispassionately.

"You look tired," he said abruptly.

Mortified, Coralie slid back on her stool and bent her head over the drawing board. Being in love was supposed to make you look radiant, wasn't it? But she had to look tired! And after the trouble she'd taken to look her best.

"How about coming across to have dinner with me this evening?" He was right by her side now, and spoke quietly, though still with a touch of weariness.

"Why, has Judith been getting on to you again?" she asked, and immediately regretted it when she looked up at him. His face seemed paler than ever

73

and the bruise made him look like the loser in a very rough fight.

"Thanks. I'd love to," she said simply.

"Come over whenever you're ready," he said shortly. "We'll dine at about eight." With that he turned and left the studio, leaving her restless and on edge. How strange that he had rushed home after saying that he would probably spend Easter in London. It must have been a terrible effort to drive the powerful two-seater all that way with a bad wrist. It was impossible to understand him. All she knew was that she was glad he was home.

Coralie took her long skirt from the wardrobe and eyed it dolefully. It was in dark-brown velvet, and well worn, but it would have to do for dinner across at the house. She had bought a silky-sherry-coloured sweater in the village, roll-necked and clinging. That would team with the skirt, and she would do things with her hair; there must be no more going round with her plait tied up in string.

Carefully she swept it up into a chignon, fastening it with an elaborate tortoiseshell comb which *Tante* Elise had sent her from Paris. Her make-up was subtle and subdued, because she couldn't bear an over-painted face. She looked into the mirror, apparently returning her own clear amber gaze, but actually seeing Scarlett again as she had seen him from her kitchen window early that afternoon.

He had been striding off alone up the rough track which led to the moors behind the house. It was raining, but he was making his way upwards to the cloud-swept heights, apparently deep in thought. There was something about the set of his shoulders which wrenched at Coralie's heart. The solitary figure seemed to her to be the real man—self-sufficient, reserved; one who kept his innermost thoughts and feelings to himself.

Of course he knew the moors intimately, had grown to manhood against their dramatic light and shade, knowing their moods. All the same Coralie eyed the black sky worriedly, and throughout the afternoon had often crossed to the studio window to look out for his return.

Whatever time he had come back she had missed him, and now she viewed her reflection dubiously. Having done her best with her appearance she resolved to forget it and try to enjoy the evening.

Judith answered the door and led her across the hall. "I've laid the table in here," she said, opening double doors, "it's cosier than the dining room."

"Cosy" was hardly the word Coralie would have used to describe the square, high-ceilinged room, but she could see what Judith meant when she saw the small round table laid for two near a glowing log fire. "Mr. Scarlett won't be a minute," said Judith. "He fell asleep in his chair in front of the fire and I hadn't the heart to wake him. He was a bit annoyed when he saw the time." Her tone made it clear that she was quite unrepentant about letting him sleep on, and after seeing Coralie settled by the fire with a drink she bustled back to the kitchen.

Coralie looked around, interested to see more of Raxhead and the furniture mentioned by Miss Silverwood. No expert on such things, she judged it to be Regency, but the room wasn't just a showcase for its contents. It looked lived-in and comfortable. Knowing his interest in design, she wondered if Scarlett was responsible for the décor and the general layout of the room. The delicate combination of turquoise, ivory, and pale gold was certainly very beautiful.

Just then he walked in, and she rose to her feet, her heart leaping uncomfortably at the sight of him. He was wearing a dark suit with a silk shirt and a rather magnificent tie. She saw that his hair was still damp, either from the rain or the bath, and that it lay close against his neck in little flat, wet rings.

She looked away quickly, aware that she had been staring far too closely, but his gaze had travelled over her just as intently, lingering on her face in much the same way it had done that first morning at the mill.

"Sorry I wasn't down when you arrived," he said, making no mention of such a human weakness as falling asleep. "I see Judith has fixed you up with a drink. Good."

He sat opposite her, where the glow from a lamp cast a decidedly sinister shadow over his bruised face. His tone was in contrast to his grim appearance, though, when he said thoughtfully, "I thought you would have gone home for Easter, Coralie. Didn't you want to?"

"Not really," she admitted candidly. "I feel I've only just settled in properly, so I don't want to leave Raxby so soon. Besides, I'm going to Liz's wedding tomorrow."

"In Leeds? Mm. You're still getting on all right with her, then? I was told she is a good worker."

"Yes, she's terrific. We get on very well together. I'm just going to watch the ceremony at the church, then I hope to do some shopping."

"You'll find excellent shops there. I'll drive you in if you like."

It was too much for Coralie. "I wouldn't dream of it," she protested firmly, in spite of the thought that she would probably dream of it all night long. "I really don't expect you to keep driving me around all over the place. I shall go by train. Perhaps before long I'll be able to buy a little old car of my own."

"Do you drive?"

She was nettled at the surprise in his tone, and answered tartly, "Yes—strange though it may seem, I do."

"Oh well, in that case take the Volvo," he said at once, referring to the estate car in which Miss Silverwood had driven her from the station. "You can have a practice run in the yard before you set off. Do you know how to find the church?"

"Well, I know how to reach it from the nearest railway station," she admitted.

Scarlett brought pen and paper and sat down beside her. As she had done in the car that day going to Miss Silverwood's, she noticed that his skin smelt fresh and very clean, but quite unperfumed with after-shave or cologne, and it pleased her. She disliked scented men.

In a moment he had drawn an easy-to-follow sketch of the road in to Leeds. "I'll get the car out of the garage for you in the morning," he offered, "and put the keys through your letter-box."

It wasn't until Judith served the first course that Coralie realised she had let herself in for driving a large and powerful car into one of the busiest cities in England. She had hardly driven at all since passing the test in her father's little Morris over four years ago. Why on earth hadn't she refused his offer?

With wide tawny eyes she watched him take his seat opposite her. He was a positive expert at getting his own way with a minimum of fuss.

She soon realised that in Judith he had a real treasure. The meal was superb and she said as much to Scarlett.

"Yes, Judith is a wonderful cook," he agreed. "She went in for domestic science and Sylvia took a secretarial course. It's rather a coincidence that they both came to work for me."

"Speaking of work, Mr. Scarlett, I've been thinking about the project . . ."

"Look, Coralie, I didn't ask you over here to talk shop."

"I'm not saying you did, but it isn't often I get the chance to talk to you alone," she pointed out, then added hurriedly, "about business, I mean, of course."

He smiled faintly. "Of course. Well, let's hear it then; what's on your mind?"

"I feel the collection would have more appeal if we included a range of silky shirts and perhaps a few long skirts in light-weight fabrics, with some evening dresses for a touch of glamour. The shirts could be in shades to match the Scarlett range, and customers could build up colour-related outfits."

"And what materials were you thinking of? Not pure silk, surely?"

"No. I thought, to begin with, really good quality synthetic knits. If they sell well then perhaps we could introduce silk later; it isn't all that expensive compared with your Scarlett prices."

"But there's the question of colour-linking . . ." He ran a lean hand through his hair and frowned thoughtfully. "None of the problems is completely insurmountable. I could get the sanction of the working committee and then the Board, I'm pretty sure, and then we could sound out the Lancashire firms. The people who are supplying the coat and skirt linings do some very good synthetics. We could approach them first. The main snag would be time. If we are to be in production by mid-June, building up stocks ready for the catalogue coming out at the end of July we should have to move quickly."

Coralie said tentatively: "I thought we could describe the polyesters as high-quality polyester jersey or whatever, "woven especially for Scarlett's." That way no other manufacturer's name need appear. Would they agree to that, do you think?"

"I don't see why not, if the price suits them," said Scarlett judiciously. "And I'm pretty sure the idea would suit Greenfield's too. Roger was hankering after more lightweights for the contract."

"Oh yes, did you hear that they had agreed to take on the making-up?"

"You know about it? Yes, Sylvie phoned me in Paris. Did Roger tell you?"

"Yes. He rang to say he was off on a tour of the E.E.C. countries."

"Mm, he was telling Sylvie about it. What happened to your date with him?" The question came suddenly, and she found herself replying meekly. "We've postponed it till he gets back."

"Good," said Scarlett calmly. "Well then, about your suggestion. Leave it with me. I'll consider it during the holiday and if I think it's a good idea we'll get moving on Tuesday. All right?"

"All right," she agreed, beaming.

"You're sure you can manage the extra work?"

"Quite sure," she said firmly.

"Right. Let's leave the subject, then, Coralie. Tell me a little about yourself, about your family. I remember you said your mother's health isn't too good, and that she trained in a Paris fashion-house. Is she French-born, then?"

"Yes. She and my father met during the war, when his plane was shot down over France. Eventually he was passed along the escape route where my mother was a courier helping airmen get back to England." Coralie tried, and failed, to keep the note of pride from her voice.

"Did he get back?" asked Scarlett with interest.

"Oh yes, in spite of being seriously ill with an infected wound. It was several years, though, before they eventually married."

"They met again after the war?"

"Yes. They had—fallen in love when they first met, but *Maman* was working for the Resistance, and father had to come back to England. He didn't know for a while that she had been taken by the Gestapo."

"My God," said Scarlett, shaken.

"She doesn't speak of what happened to her, but when she was released her health was broken. When she and my father had parted they promised to wait for each other no matter what happened. The war finished, but my father was ill and had very little money, but at last he went over to France and found her. She had waited for him, but—things happened, and it was a few years before he could bring her back here. She wasn't well; her lungs had been affected, and she would not agree to marry until she was in better health.

"In the end, when she was almost thirty they were married and a few years later I was born. They were very happy. My father died four years ago of a heart attack."

"They sound a wonderful couple," said Scarlett, and she wondered if it was a wistfulness in his voice.

"Yes," she said simply.

"And what about you, Coralie? Are you like your parents? Will you marry for love? Do you even believe in such a thing?"

She lowered her lashes quickly. "Yes," she replied guardedly. "I believe in love. I think it's the only real basis for marriage, and I certainly wouldn't marry without it."

"And what about your career? Where does that come in your scheme of things?"

"Well, of course, I want to make a success of my career, but if it came to a choice between that and a happy marriage then I'm afraid the career would have to go."

For a moment he was silent, then he said, "I see. You're not exactly a militant feminist, are you, Coralie?"

"Not really," she agreed with a smile. "I like women to be women and men to be men without too much mixing up of their rôles. I suppose I'm old-fashioned, but I can't help that."

Unconsciously adding weight to her words she jumped up to help Judith when she came in to clear the table. "That was a wonderful meal, Judith," she said sincerely. "The best I've eaten for ages."

A small smile was allowed to appear above Judith's ample chins. "I should hope you've not been neglecting your food, the way you've been working, my girl," she said severely. "I've told Mr. Scarlett time and again that you're overdoing it and that you need good, nourishing food." With that she marched off, pushing her trolley before her like a devoted nanny with her pram.

"Judith likes you, that's evident," he said, as Coralie sat down again.

"I'm not too sure about that," she replied doubtfully. "She's always telling me off."

"That proves it. She only tells off those she likes. To anyone else she's merely polite."

From then on the talk between them drifted from one thing to another. She thought often of her plan to be cool, efficient and friendly; but she asked herself helplessly how she could be cool when the human dynamo was switched to "charm," and generating that captivating quality at full power? How could she display efficiency when she was not allowed to discuss work? It was all too easy, though, to be friendly when Scarlett was such entertaining company, and her laugh rang out time and again, causing Judith and Walter to exchange glances as they went up to bed.

Coralie had been watching the time, anxious not to outstay her welcome and conscious that Scarlett must be exhausted. At eleven, she said, "I think I should be going, Mr. Scarlett, it's getting late."

"Surely you don't need to go yet," he asked, surprised.

"But you tell me I look tired," she pointed out reasonably, "so I must need more sleep."

"You always have an answer, don't you?" He smiled lazily, and she thought she had never seen him look more relaxed. "Thanks for an enjoyable evening, Coralie. Please come again."

"Thank you! I've enjoyed it as well."

"Oh, I almost forgot." He crossed to a small table and picked up a package. "Here's a little present from Paris."

"For me?" She was touched, and for one awful moment felt as if she might cry.

"Well go on, open it. If I'd know for certain you were half-French I would have chosen it in fear and trembling."

The idea of him doing anything at all in fear and trembling was so ludicrous she started to laugh again, while Scarlett watched her, half-smiling.

The heavy embossed wrapping paper revealed a similarly embossed box. Inside was a chunky gold-stoppered bottle of perfume—Worth's *Fleurs Fraiches.*

"Mr. Scarlett, it's lovely, but I can't, I mean—I don't think—well, thank you very much."

He cut short her confused words. "The pleasure is mine, I assure you, Coralie. I have no idea what it smells like. I bought it because of the name—it reminded me of you."

Fleurs Fraiches—Fresh Flowers. She looked up into his face, feeling completely at a loss, and bit her lip. "Thank you," she whispered at last, and clasping the box in both hands, made for the door.

He was there before her, and led her across the hall. "Good-night, Coralie," he said gently, helping her into the despised coat, but mercifully making no comment about it.

"Good-night, Mr. Scarlett, and thank you again."

She turned to go, but his hand on her arm stayed her.

"Could you, do you think, abandon the 'Mr. Scarlett'? My name is Jethro, as I'm sure you know. Keep to Mr. Scarlett at the mill, if you must, but up here—"

"All right. I'll try. Good-night again—Jethro."

"That's it. Not too difficult, after all, is it?" With a hint of that devastating smile he sent her on her way, and remained standing in the lighted doorway until she reached the top of the stairs. He returned her wave, and for some reason was still there watching when she went in and closed the door behind her.

Six

Coralie sat in a back pew, watching the guests arrive and absorbing the tranquility of the old church. The organ was playing softly, and fitful sunbeams shone through the stained glass windows, lighting the arrangements of yellow and white spring flowers.

The sixty-mile journey from Raxby had been surprisingly easy after the first nerve-wracking moments of handling the big car. As Scarlett had promised, it was waiting for her in the courtyard early that morning, and the keys had been put through her letter-box.

He himself was nowhere to be seen, which she found rather a relief as she thought she might make a hash of driving the Volvo.

Carefully she examined the controls and drove a slow circuit of the courtyard, then more boldly out along the wide track which cut across the face of the hill. Slowly she reversed and turned in the entrance to a field then drove back past Raxhead and made her triumphant but cautious way down to the road. The run to Leeds had been quite straightforward after that, and the sequence of busy road junctions on the outskirts had given her no difficulty.

Thoughtfully she looked back on the previous evening. What astoundingly good company Scarlett had been. How completely charming he could be when he felt like it—no wonder he was never short of female company.

Then her thoughts were whisked away from Scarlett. The bride had arrived, and with a tightening of the throat Coralie rose to her feet with the rest of the congregation as Liz walked up the aisle on her father's arm.

She was not really a pretty girl, with her little snub nose and chubby face, but she looked quite lovely in her bridal white, with her bright hair gleaming through the veil, and her curvy figure given a new dignity by the fall of the classically simple gown. Coralie cast an interested and professional eye at the back view, knowing that Liz had made the dress herself. Typically, it was a perfect fit, the train sweeping evenly and easily over the red carpet of the aisle.

The bridesmaids, two teenage cousins of Liz, were in dresses of pale green voile, and carried posies of yellow and white daisies, echoing the colours of the daffodils and narcissi which decorated the church.

As the beautiful words of the wedding service reached her Coralie became conscious of an odd little ache in her breast; a tightening deep inside her in the region of her heart. Somewhere, just recently, she had experienced that same feeling—where had it been, and when?

"I, Elizabeth, take thee, Robert, to my lawful wedded husband, for richer, for poorer . . ."

Now, watching as Rob bent his dark head closer to Liz's shining coppery curls, Coralie admitted, just for one brief moment, that she felt envious of Liz standing at the altar with the man she loved, while she, Coralie, was merely striving for friendship with the man who held her heart in the hollow of his capable hand.

Then she firmly dismissed such feelings. The fact that he had asked her views on marriage was no reason for getting all emotional about it. Still, it had seemed that he was sounding her out about it for some reason of his own. . . .

With a small smile at her own foolishness Coralie watched as Liz, pink-cheeked and radiant, walked down the aisle on her husband's arm. Then hurriedly she followed them outside, her bag of confetti ready for when the photographs were finished.

It had been a lovely wedding, and she was glad she had made the effort to go, she thought as she ate a lunch-time snack in a snack bar. The Volvo was safe and sound in a car park, and she was eager to set off and explore the shops.

As Scarlett had said, Leeds was an excellent shopping centre, and the time flew past as she looked for material for the evening dress. It was no use, she simply could not bring herself to buy a ready-made one when she could design and sew an original at a fraction of the cost.

In the end she chose a silky jersey fabric in a misty sea-green. It would suit her unusual colouring, and would look good throughout the year if she made a separate top to go over it for colder weather.

Pleased with her purchase, and in search of a light-weight sweater, Coralie made her way along the thronged pavement. A few yards in front of her a tall dark-haired man and a slim, fashionably-dressed woman were leaving a small jeweller's shop. The woman was instantly recognisable as Janice Ellison, but it was her escort who held Coralie's gaze. Not surprisingly, it was Jethro Scarlett.

The pair of them seemed to be in high spirits, and as Coralie followed a few paces behind them Janice stretched up on tiptoe and kissed him warmly on the cheek. The afternoon crowds surged on, oblivious to such an everyday gesture, but Coralie wasn't in the least oblivious. She gasped, the breath escaping from her as if she had been punched in the midriff, then she turned and walked hurriedly away in the opposite direction, her thoughts in chaos.

After a few moments she slowed down, her common sense reasserting itself. Why the heavy drama? Nothing earth-shaking had happened; nothing unexpected, come to that. It was probably a kiss of thanks for some gift or other—after all, they had just been in a jeweller's shop, and a pretty expensive one, by the look of it.

Coralie's step faltered. A jeweller's shop? Necklaces—bracelets—rings—. An engagement ring, perhaps? All pleasure in the afternoon gone, Coralie made for the car-park, her search for a sweater forgotten. She would have to be making for Raxby soon, in any case, if she was to be back before dark.

She straightened the little green cap to an unwittingly ferocious angle as she approached the car, then for a moment leaned back in the seat before starting the engine, her face softening. He had looked very happy as he came out of the shop with Janice. . . .

By nine-thirty the next morning she was sewing the sea-green dress. Already she had been down to Raxby church for Easter communion, and as she walked back up the lane pale sunshine was washing the hillside with silver. The unmistakable smell of spring was in the air, and in spite of her sober thoughts Coralie's spirits rose with some of her old light-hearted optimism.

She decided to move the dining table over to the big window and do her machining there. The light would be better and she could look out and see the sunlight patterning the hills as the white puff-ball clouds raced overhead.

She had designed the dress in a simple Grecian style, cut on the bias, with one shoulder left bare. It was a style where the cut was everything, and without a lot of complicated sewing to do. The jacket was a straight, long-sleeved affair with a softly-tied neckline, equally simple and quick to make.

It went well, and by tea-time the dress was almost finished. She tried it on again and felt fairly satisfied. The material was rather more clinging than she had anticipated, and outlined her figure sharply in spite of the draped front. But the general effect was just what she had aimed for. She could wear her hair in Grecian style as well, swept up and back into waves and tendrils, and threaded with ribbons or beads.

It was quite a novelty to be making something so glamorous for herself, not to menton a bit of a let-down if Roger took her to some sleazy little disco! But she felt stiff and a little bit tired as she pulled her jeans back on. It was still light outside, so wearing the blanket-cloth coat she set off for a quick walk across the hillside.

To her disappointment the air felt cold and clammy, quite unlike the freshness of the morning, but with her thoughts already on the well-worn theme of Scarlett and Janice she made her way along the wide track across the face of the hill. It would peter out eventually, she thought, or lead to some remote farm, but as long as it didn't climb up to the moors she would be quite safe when dark-ness fell.

Down below in the valley she could see the mill, its tall, rather graceful chimney for once without its wisp of smoke; and winding around the mill buildings was the little river, looking dull and leaden beneath the darkening sky.

From her high vantage point she could see Miss Silverwood's house, snug against the rising ground which closed off the end of the valley. In the opposite direction, right away on the other side of the village, was the stone cottage where Liz and Rob would live. She was sure she could see it in the middle of a row of similar cottages, all belonging to Scarlett. Liz had taken her back there one evening to have a meal with Rob and herself, and to show her the work they had done on the house.

Coralie leaned on the cold stones of the wall bordering the track, disturbing a solitary sheep which ran bleating back to the flock, its heavy fleece beaded with moisture. She shivered as she stood there, dreaming, and put up her hood. The little house had been newly-decorated and shining, evidence that Liz and Rob had worked hard to have everything ready before the wedding.

Of course, recalled Coralie suddenly, that was when she had first felt that odd little ache in her heart, when she was being shown over the house by a very proud Liz! The same ache which she had been unable to ignore during the wedding ceremony. She sighed and stood upright, but when she turned homewards the lights of Raxhead seemed dim and very far away. Uneasily she looked behind her and saw the mist swirling down rapidly from the moor.

On the other side of the wall the group of sheep moved together quickly, their long solemn faces expressionless and rather sinister as the last fading light caught their eyes.

Thank goodness she had not left the track. Hastily she retraced her steps, astonished to find that she stumbled frequently because she couldn't see a yard in front of her, and in fact could not even see her own two feet on the ground.

The silence was absolute, even her footsteps on the stony track were silent. But she realised that it didn't feel hard beneath her feet. It was tussocky and springy. Unbelievingly she bent to feel the ground. It was grassland—a field! Or was she, perhaps, up on the edge of the moor, having wandered through a gap in the wall?

But it was ridiculous. She had been within sight of the house, almost within calling distance, and now she was stumbling about, completely lost, only a couple of hundred yards away from Raxhead.

The obvious thing to do was to stay where she was until the mist lifted, but it was intensely cold, and to stand and wait like a fool didn't appeal to Coralie at all. She would try to find the dry-stone wall which bordered the track, then follow it for some distance, and if it didn't take her back to the house she would turn back and go in the opposite direction.

For what seemed an eternity she stumbled around helplessly. She was being foolish, she knew that, and at last she sank down beside a huge boulder and drew the coat more closely about her. Nobody knew where she was, of course, so nobody would come to look for her. Would she be all right if the mist stayed until morning? It was quite unbelievably cold, and already her feet in the unlined leather boots were numb. If she had known Yorkshire would be like this she would have taken a crash course in survival before she came to Raxby, she thought grimly.

But the damp and the cold and the impenetrable darkness were telling on her nerves, and in spite of her efforts at self-control an overwrought sob escaped her as she stamped her feet wearily and swung her arms back and forth.

It was with a blissful sensation of relief that she heard her name called.

"Over here," she shouted shakily, forcing herself to keep still. "Over here."

It was Scarlett, of course, though how he had known where to find her she couldn't attempt to guess.

"Coralie! You little fool!" With that tender greeting the man she loved appeared in front of her, his hair plastered wetly across his forehead. Walter hovered anxiously at his side, carrying an enormous torch.

She gaped up at Scarlett, weak with relief, but to her horror he grabbed her by the shoulders and shook her violently. "Idiot!" he snarled furiously. "I told you these hills were dangerous." His hands bit deeply into her flesh through the cheap cloth of her coat.

But Coralie was in no mood to be chastised and shaken. "Take your hands off me, you great bully," she cried furiously. "How did I know the mist would come down like a blanket? I didn't get lost on purpose!" With a weak slap she tried to knock his hands from her shoulders, and to her everlasting shame burst into tears.

"Happen we should get her back home, Mr. Scarlett," broke in Walter, the light from the torch showing an astonished gleam in his eyes.

All at once she was lifted off her feet with effortless ease as Scarlett took her up in his arms. Walter lit the way ahead, and as rapidly as if they were on a town pavement the two men walked unerringly over the rough ground. It seemed an awfully long time before they were back on the track, but she was too worn out to care. The indignity of being carried like a child in his arms gave way to a sense of pleasure so acute that her icy body seemed to melt with the delightful warmth of his closeness.

She stole a glance up at him, but it was too dark to see more than the outline of his jaw.

"I'm all right now, thank you," she said meekly. "I'll walk."

For all the notice he took she might not have spoken. He walked on, her weight troubling him not at all. In a couple of minutes they were at the staircase to her flat, confirming her reasoning that Raxhead had all the time been very near. He made no attempt to put her down, so she wriggled violently. "Put me down! Please!"

Strong arms just held her more firmly, and as Walter went back to the house Scarlett carried her up the stairs and into the flat, dumping her none too gently on the rug by the door.

He switched on the light and for the first time she was able to take a good look at his face. He was a ghastly colour, with the bruise showing up black and green against the grey skin. For a moment he looked down at her as she stood woebegone and wet with her hair tangled across her face. The startlingly blue gaze showed no signs of softening, nor did he speak, but marched into her bathroom and turned on the taps at full power.

"Hot bath," he instructed briefly. "Then get into bed."

When she remained where she was, just gazing at him as if mesmerised, he calmly unfastened her coat, removed it, and pushed her roughly in the direction of the bathroom. Fury boiled in Coralie again. If he bullied her any more she would surely slap his face and put another bruise next to the beauty he already had.

When she emerged, pink and thawed out and wearing her towelling robe he was nowhere to be seen. Thank goodness for that, she thought in relief, going to the kitchen for a drink.

But he was there before her, pouring hot milk into a beaker. "Bed!" he said decisively, as though to a disobedient six-year-old.

She stared at him again, her lower lip thrust out mutinously. Why was he in such a rage? It wasn't as if she'd been stupid enough to wander for miles over the moors. Had she perhaps spoiled his evening? And in any case, how had he known where she was?

With that uncanny facility for reading her mind he said: "Walter saw you set off, but he never thought you'd be fool enough to linger out there with the mist coming down."

Once more she felt the onset of foolish tears, and she certainly wasn't going to let him see her weeping again, so with great dignity she marched off to the bedroom, her hair swathed in a towel.

Hardly had she put on her nightie and climbed wearily into bed before he tapped at the door and brought in the hot milk. A sense of unreality enveloped her. This was her employer who was warming milk for her and waiting on her. It was a little unnerving to have him dashing in and out of her bedroom like a male nurse.

Her voice was strained when she said: "Thank you. And thanks for finding me and bringing me back." She raised weary eyes to his, her invariable honesty compelling her to ask, "But why are you so furious? Have I spoiled your evening? If so, I'm sorry."

He stared at her incredulously, and she wriggled uneasily in her skimpy cotton nightie. "Of course you've spoiled my evening," he said distinctly. "And it would have spoiled the entire night if I'd gone on searching and eventually found a corpse. Do you realise if Walter hadn't seen you set off you might have been dead of exposure by morning? And you ask if you've spoiled my evening!" Heavily he turned to the door. "Go to sleep, Coralie. Go to sleep."

A moment later she heard him enter the kitchen to get his coat. Stunned, she repeated to herself: "Dead? Dead of exposure?" Oh dear Heaven, how could she have forgotten? She had resurrected a ghost for him, the ghost of the girl who had died out on those same moors.

"Mr. Scarlett," she called. "Mr. Scarlett, wait!" She grabbed her robe and threw it hurriedly over her shoulders. The towel fell from her hair but she left it on the floor. She found him standing by the door, already pressing the handle.

"I've just realised why you are so upset," she said rapidly. "How can I ever apologise for—for bringing it all back?"

He made no pretence of not knowing what she meant, but the taut line of his lips eased by a fraction. He didn't speak.

"Truly, I never imagined I would get lost so near the house. I only went out for a ten-minute walk. I never intended to upset you. . . ."

"It's all right, Coralie." The deep voice was gentle at last, but a deathly weariness lay on the dark features. "I'm sorry too, for shaking you and bullying you and—frightening you."

"But I know the reason for it now," she pointed out, then before she could prevent the words escaping her, she asked, "Did you love her very much?"

"Yes," he said simply. "I loved her." And with that he opened the door and went out.

Days later, as the pressure of work at the studio increased, the events of the Easter weekend took on the quality of a remembered nightmare. So much had happened in so short a time, from the news of the plane crash right through to the painful moment when Scarlett admitted he had loved the girl who died on the moors.

During a restless night she had resolved to try to recapture the easy friendship which they had shared so briefly when they had dined together. But there had been no opportunity to attempt this on Easter Monday, because at eight a.m. she had seen him drive off in the two-seater, and it had been after midnight when he returned. It didn't take too much cudgelling of her brains to conclude that he had been with Janice once more.

As for her suspicion that they were now engaged, there had been no mention of it from anyone at the mill, no confirmation of it in any of the daily papers which she had examined during the last ten days. Even Judith Braithwaite had thrown no light on the matter when Coralie had brought up Janice's name during a shared coffee in the kitchen at Raxhead.

"Oh, Mr. Scarlett has known the Ellisons all his life," said the housekeeper. "He used to play with Janice when they were children. Mr. Scarlett and Mr. Ralph used to go off over the top to the Ellison place, and leave little Helen crying because she was too small to go with them, and then Mr. Ralph would tease her for being a cry-baby. My mother was the cook here for years, and she used to tell me what the boys had been up to."

And that fascinating glimpse of the past was all that Judith had to offer. If she had formed any views on the present-day relationship between Scarlett and Janice she was obviously not going to share them.

Coralie found that, true to his promise, Scarlett must have given some thought to her suggestion of incorporating light-weights in the collection. On Tuesday morning he rang the studio to tell her that after sounding out the Board he had decided to go ahead with the idea, and that he was about to contact Newbitt's in Manchester about the polyesters.

A week later batches of samples arrived at the studio for her approval. "What do you think of them?" asked Scarlett on his early morning visit to the studio. "I have no real worries about the colour-linking—the lab technicians will take care of that without too much trouble. What I really want to know is—are you happy with the quality?"

"Oh, yes," she assured him. "It will make up beautifully."

For a moment silence fell between them, and her gaze strayed to the superb silver-grey worsted suit he was wearing. It was a fresh, sunny morning, and she thought he must have dressed in the belief that spring had finally arrived. The silence lengthened, and she found herself wishing that Liz was back at work. Her cheerful, down-to-earth presence would surely have helped to dispel the constraint which descended on Coralie whenever Scarlett paid one of his lightning visits to the studio.

"I've been thinking that it would be a good idea for you to go over to Manchester to see the range of patterns that Newbitt's are designing for us," he said at last. "You could chat to their design team, and choose whatever you like for the evening dresses and skirts, on my authority. Then I'll tell the production boys to check with Greenfield's and work out how much we need to order."

"Oh," said Coralie, rather overcome. "Of course I'll go over to Manchester any time you say."

"The sooner the better," he said briefly. "I've arranged for you to have a company car from now on. You will have to work closely with Greenfield's until production starts, and that will mean visiting Leeds from time to time. Add to that the odd trip to Manchester and it becomes quite clear that you need your own transport. You'll find a Mini waiting for you in the works garage. It's yours for as long as you stay with the firm, and a new one every two years."

With a grin at her astonished expression and a dismissive wave of the hand at her thanks he strode off rapidly on his morning tour of the mill. From the studio door Coralie watched his tall, grey-clad figure out of sight. Then she took a deep breath. A company car! Her fortunes had changed with a vengeance since that afternoon at the Dorchester. Five thousand a year, a super rent-free flat—and now a Mini of her own. She had risen in the world since the days when she sat at the register in Benson's Save-all Supermarket.

With an excited little laugh she picked up her shears and cut into a length of rose-pink woolen hopsack. Some time later the studio phone rang. "Mr. Greenfield for you, Miss Dee," said the switchboard girl.

"Hello, Roger," she said, surprised. "I didn't think you'd be back yet."

"I'm not," he laughed. "I'm in Amsterdam at the moment. I just thought I'd ring to tell you to keep Saturday night free for our date. I shall be home sooner than I thought."

Coralie's eyes widened. It was Thursday already, and didn't he mean "ask" not "tell"?

"Hello, Coralie? Is that all right? You'll come out with me on Saturday?"

She swallowed her misgivings. It was typical of

his assertive personality that he should take it for granted that she would be available.

"Yes, that's fine, Roger," she answered serenely. "Where shall I see you?"

"At your place, of course. I'll pick you up at 7:30. Wear your best bib and tucker and I'll think of somewhere decent to take you." Then he said, with a subtle difference in tone, "Thanks for doing your stuff with J.J., by the way. I've just been chatting with him and he told me you'd talked him into it."

"Doing my stuff?" she echoed.

"Yes. I'm glad I mentioned to you that we would be pleased to have some light-weights included in the contract. It will suit our programme of work so much better to have both the light and heavy machinists working on Scarlett's stuff simultaneously. Anyway, thanks a lot. I never forget a favour, Coralie. See you Saturday."

With those surprising words he rang off, the brash confident tones echoing in her ears long after she had replaced the receiver.

Coralie stared at the instrument uneasily. A favour? He had obviously taken it for granted that she had persuaded Scarlett to include the light-weights just because he, Roger, had wanted it. Vaguely she recalled him mentioning this point when they discussed her designs the day they came back to the studio from Scarlett's office. And with her usual honesty she admitted now that his remark had probably triggered off her own ideas of having silky shirts and dresses in the collection. But to take it for granted that she had done it specially for him—he must be mad!

Another thought struck her, and she almost groaned aloud. Had Roger perhaps hinted as much to Scarlett? The thought that he should mistake her motives was to much to tolerate! Hastily she picked up the phone.

"Miss Silverwood? Coralie here. Could I possibly

come to see Mr. Scarlett for a few minutes? Is he free? Oh, good. I'll come right away."

Still in her yellow smock she rushed along the corridor, uncertain what she was going to say to him, but quite determined to clear up any wrong ideas on his part.

She found him behind a littered desk, with Miss Silverwood typing rapidly in the outer office. He was in his shirt sleeves. A silk shirt, it was true, with heavy gold cuff-links, and worn with one of his superb ties, but he looked hard-pressed and just the tiniest bit harassed. The spectacular bruise was at last fading, she noticed with relief.

"I'm sorry to bother you," she began, then stopped. The disconcerting stare was fixed on her flushed face.

"That's all right, Coralie. What's on your mind?"

"I've just been talking to Roger Greenfield, and he seemed to think that I persuaded you to include the polyesters just to please him, because he had mentioned it to me that day when he came here."

The slightest smile softened the firm mouth. "Mm. And what did you say to that?"

"Well, nothing really. He rang off before I could reply. It was only when I'd hung up that it dawned on me what he was on about. I—I couldn't help wondering if he'd hinted as much to you."

"As a matter of fact he didn't," said Scarlett calmly. "Though I can't imagine why you should think I'd go along with the idea, anyway. But now that you're here, tell me, did what he said influence your thinking on the matter?"

"Well—I think perhaps his remark may have started me thinking along those lines—but that's all. I would never dream of asking for such a major change just to benefit Greenfield's."

He didn't reply to that, but merely nodded, looking at her with that considering expression on his face, leaning back in his chair and swivelling it slowly

97

from side to side. There seemed to be no point in prolonging the interview, so she said lamely, "Well, that's all I came to say."

"Thanks, Coralie. Your concern does you credit." He rose from the chair and came round the desk to face her. "But for your information I would not have paid much attention even if Roger had spelled out his version to me in words of one syllable. You forget—I've known him for a very long time. And even more important, I know you as well. I think your loyalty to Scarlett's and the success of the project would mean more to you than what Roger wants or doesn't want. Am I right?"

"Yes," she breathed.

"I thought so. Now, are you free on Saturday evening? I'd like to take you out to dinner, if by any chance that appeals to you."

Coralie looked down at the carpet in embarrassment. If it appealed to her! "Saturday," she repeated. "I'm sorry. I'm going out for the evening. Perhaps another time?"

After his remarks about her loyalty to the firm she was reluctant to tell him who her date was with. But suppose Scarlett was somewhere around when Roger came to pick her up. Hastily she added, "Roger asked me just now, on the phone."

"I see," said Scarlett quietly. "As I said once before, he always was a quick worker. Well, perhaps some other time."

Dismissing her without the need of words, he picked up a file, and opening it, scanned the contents. With a final glance at the bent dark head Coralie left the office, directing only a wan smile at Miss Silverwood as she went.

She collected the car when she finished work that evening. It was a white Mini, and she had to admit to a real thrill when Bill, the garage foreman, put the keys into her hand. A few minutes later she parked on the grass verge and dashed into the phone box. "What do you think, *Maman*, I've been given a company car—a brand-new Mini. It's mine for as long as I stay with Scarlett's. Isn't it *fantastic*? No, of course I'm not thinking of leaving, not for ages and ages or until I'm fired! Have you thought over what I suggested about coming to see me? The weather is improving at last, and we've actually seen the sun once or twice. If you leave it just a little bit longer, say until the middle of May, it should be warmer for you. What do you say?"

Coralie waited anxiously for a reply. She missed Francine, and was constantly in fear of her over-doing things while she was away.

"The shop is closing for a week at the beginning of June, because the painters are coming in," said her mother thoughtfully. "I could come then without having to take time off whilst they are open."

"Great! We'll fix up about the journey nearer the time. And when you're here I shall be able to drive you around the district in my Mini."

Coralie rang off and drove up the lane to Raxhead. There was room to garage her car next to the Volvo without encroaching on the space for Scarlett's two-seater, and she gave the little car a loving pat before she left it.

That evening she went to the studio across at the house. She liked working there on her designs for the evening dresses and skirts, finding that the change in surroundings was helpful when she wanted to switch her mind from the rest of the collection.

She had brought a wad of samples home with her earlier in the week, and now she turned them over thoughtfully. If she had seen the printed light-weights she would be far better equipped to design the dresses. Scarlett had said "go to Manchester as soon as possible," so on impulse, she decided to go the next day. Thoughtfully she pinned a pencilled sketch to the easel and took out her water-colours.

One sketch led to another and the hours flew past. Occasionally she rubbed her aching back and wriggled stiff shoulders, and when she stopped she found to her astonishment that it was past midnight. Her head ached, she felt as stiff as a board, and she was ravenously hungry.

She stacked the sketches, knowing that some of them were good, in fact better than anything she had done so far. She let herself out of the studio quietly, wary of disturbing Judith and Walter. Knowing the sort of hours Jethro Scarlett kept, she was sure there was little likelihood of wakening him because he wouldn't yet be asleep.

Wearily she climbed the stairs to the flat. Perhaps he was right and she was overdoing it a bit. And what a fool she was to work so late the night before the long drive to Manchester! She switched on the fire and went into the kitchen to make herself a sandwich and a cup of Bovril.

She felt a little better with the pangs of hunger satisfied and lay back for a moment against the plump cushions of the settee. Had she been right to tell Scarlett that her date on Saturday was with Roger? Subterfuge didn't come easily to her, and although she had been reluctant to tell him, it had been easier than facing up to the possible complications of keeping it from him.

Suddenly, without any change in her position, Coralie fell into the deep, coma-like sleep of exhaustion, the warmth of the room and the comfort of the settee combining to keep her undisturbed.

She was wakened by a loud knocking at the door, and with a shock realised that she was lying fully-dressed on the settee. The living-room lights were on, even though it was broad daylight outside, and the room was overpoweringly hot.

Before she could gather her wits the door was unlocked and Scarlett came in, stopping abruptly when he saw her lying on the settee.

"What's wrong? Are you not well? I saw the lights on and your car in the garage, and as it's nearly ten I became concerned, so I borrowed Judith's key and came in." He moved his shoulders uneasily, "I'm sorry to barge in on you like this—"

"Ten o'clock!" gasped Coralie. "But it can't be! I have to go to Manchester today." She swung her feet to the floor.

"You will do no such thing," he said decisively. "By the looks of it you were too tired to go to bed last night—oh yes, I know it was after midnight when you left the studio—and in that case I can't have you driving all that way."

"But I thought you said I should go as soon as possible?"

"Yes, I think you should," he admitted, "Newbitt's are waiting for you to choose your designs so that they can go into production on them. As a favour to us, of course. They don't usually produce fabrics to order at such short notice." He paused for a moment. "How do you feel?"

"All right," she said untruthfully. "Really I do."

"Well, if you're sure of that I'll drive you over there myself. It will be a break from the infernal studios for you. Besides, I need to talk to George Newbitt, and I'd like to have a look at their designs as well."

Coralie's heart began to thump uncomfortably. Did he really have to go or was he feeling the urge to play male nurse again?

"But can you spare the time away from the mill?" she asked, remembering his littered desk and shirt-sleeves the day before.

"I think I can manage it," he said imperturbably. "Ring the doorbell at the house when you're ready to set off, and not before you've had a decent breakfast, either."

When he had gone Coralie took a quick bath and made herself some toast and a boiled egg. What on earth was he doing at home at ten o'clock in the morning? Everybody knew he was always at his desk by eight-thirty. Still puzzling, she hastily swallowed her breakfast and went to brush her teeth. A careful make-up would have to go by the board, she decided, giving her lips just a touch of her favourite lipstick. On impulse she dabbed a touch of the precious *Fleurs Fraiches* in the hollow of her throat and quickly finished dressing.

It was going to be a day for her leather hat. She would need all the confidence she could muster.

Seven

They hadn't even left Raxby before he tackled her about overworking.

"Now, Coralie, let's have a discussion about your working hours. You can't go on like this—working until after midnight and then falling asleep before you can get into bed. You'll make yourself ill. It's got to stop because I simply will not allow it."

When she didn't reply he looked across at her and asked, "What's wrong?"

"If that's the prelude to a discussion," she said simply, "it's the oddest one I've ever heard. You seem to have made up your mind without me saying a word."

He laughed at that. "Well, perhaps it was more a declaration of intent than anything. I intend to see that you slow down a little. You're well up to date with the designs and Liz is due back on Monday, so what is it that's goading you on to such a punishing schedule?"

"I don't know," she admitted helplessly. "I can't seem to relax in the evenings without thinking of the designs, and then I just have to get them down on paper. Last night I didn't notice the time passing because the evening dresses were coming on well."

"Will you promise me that you won't even put pencil to paper during the weekend, and that on Monday you'll work from nine till five and not a minute longer? Actually I think you should have a

103

complete rest for a few days but that's too much to ask, I suppose?"

"You mean take time off?" She was shocked. "Oh, I couldn't possibly. I'm far too busy, and besides I enjoy going to work too much to stay at home. You're paying me a good salary, and I intend to earn it."

"I don't think there's any doubt that you're doing that, Coralie," he said quietly, changing gear as they climbed up into the Pennines. She shot him a look then, her eyes wide beneath the long lashes. Yes, he seemed to mean it. Suddenly her heart sang, and the tiredness that had bedevilled her fell away. She was out for the day with him, just the two of them together. And he had admitted that she was earning her money, so he must be pleased with her work. Happiness filled her, but she sat demurely at his side, and just tilted the leather hat to a slightly more rakish angle.

"In a minute you'll have a good view," he said as they took a sharp bend.

He slowed the car, and she saw down below them a peaceful little dale, basking in the pale sunshine. A narrow river tumbled hurriedly over its rocky bed between damp green meadows lying like quilted silk across the valley floor. The great hills rose and curved on either side until they reached the wild untended moors, and Coralie turned in her seat to look behind them. For as far as the eye could see there was rough, undulating moorland, serrated by deep gullies and broken by gaunt, weather-worn rocks. The contrast between that desolate landscape and the tranquil little dale was spellbinding.

"It's lovely, isn't it, Jethro?" she breathed, and then blushed vividly. For the first time of her own accord, but quite unintentionally, she had used his Christian name.

In answer the brilliant smile lit his dark features, but he made no comment, just nodding his head as he looked at her intently. "Lovely," he agreed.

After that he said little, apparently having no desire to discuss work, and she sat at his side in contented silence, watching the changing scenery as they came down from the hills. Presently they joined the motorway, and before long entered the vast urban sprawl of Greater Manchester.

"Do you know this part of the country?" he asked.

"No, not at all. But there seem to be plenty of those 'dark satanic mills' around," she smiled.

Newbitt's was an enormous place, surrounded by numerous buildings and workshops. Scarlett led her to George Newbitt's office, where the elderly manufacturer welcomed him warmly.

"Jethro, my lad, you're looking well." He looked at Coralie appraisingly. "Still picking the pretty ones, eh?"

"Jethro my lad" smiled briefly. "This one has brains as well, George. Meet Coralie Dee, our designer for the ready-to-wear. As I said on the phone, she's here to make her choice from your new designs."

Newbitt's shrewd grey eyes seemed to estimate her ability as they shook hands, and he nodded as if satisfied at what he saw. He called to a girl in the outer office. "Take Miss Dee to Design, please," he said, "and you must go along and see what we've dreamed up for you after we've had our chat, Jethro."

Scarlett went with him and Coralie followed her guide to the Design Department. For the next half hour she had a marvellous time. Two middle-aged men and a younger woman constituted the team, and Coralie found it a great boost to her morale to be accepted as an equal by the three experienced designers.

She saw for herself how their original coloured designs had become the lovely printed polyesters which were swirled and draped over a small display stand awaiting her arrival. The reproduction wasn't perfect, as these were only experimental lengths, but even so she was impressed by the lovely subtle colours.

Some of the designs she was able to reject at once. They just didn't fit her mental picture of the Scarlett collection at all. Others she put on one side for consideration, and two she chose immediately; one a swirly abstract design in warm gold and russet tones which she felt would be a winner for an autumn and winter catalogue, and the other in dull pink, patterned with skeletal branches and long wispy leaves.

In all she had to choose six, and as she decided on the last one Scarlett joined her. He said little, but she thought he seemed relieved by the sight of the beautiful fabrics. He examined the ones she had chosen and said, "Yes, I like them. They're good. And I've arranged with George that they'll be exclusive to us."

Then he turned to the designers, admiring their current work and chatting knowledgeably with them. He really knows his stuff, thought Coralie with a ridiculous surge of pride. He seems to be as much at home with synthetics as he is with his own pure wools.

At last they left, both highly pleased with the visit.

"Food next," said Scarlett firmly. "Are you hungry? Good. So am I. I know a decent place just off St. Ann's Square where we'll be in time for a late lunch."

With his usual expertise he drove rapidly into the city itself and straight to a small restaurant. It had a quietly luxurious air, but even so Coralie was stunned when she caught sight of the prices.

Sitting across the table from Scarlett inevitably recalled their shared dinner on Good Friday, and Coralie was glad that they seemed to have regained the easy companionship which they had enjoyed then. The intensity of the night she had been lost might have been a particularly unnerving dream.

She couldn't help watching him as their first

course was served. He was really astonishingly attractive, with his lean tanned features and arresting blue eyes. The silver-grey suit had the effect of enhancing his dark good looks, making him stand out in comparison to the other more soberly-clad men in the room; for the first time in her life Coralie felt the thrill of being seen in public with a man who drew admiring glances as inevitably as a magnet attracts iron.

He himself appeared to be quite unaware of it, eating his soup with enjoyment and not noticing the interested glances of two well-dressed women nearby. But Coralie was conscious of observing everything in the minutest detail. The fine dark hairs on the back of his wrists; his very white, slightly uneven teeth, the way his voice sank even deeper when he spoke to her quietly across the table. Their surroundings too were affecting her, so that she felt she would remember forever the brass bowl filled with daffodils on the low window-ledge at her side, the dull sheen of the wood-panelling around the room, and the distant steady murmur of the city traffic.

They had finished their main course when three women dressed in ultra-fashionable style entered the restaurant.

"Darling!" With a little whoop of joy one of them came across to their table, and with a shock Coralie saw that it was Janice, complete with a frizzy auburn wig, and wearing an outfit which seemed to consist of khaki-drill decorated with corset-lacing.

Scarlett rose to his feet and Janice kissed him lightly on the lips. It may have been an innocent greeting but the sight of it cut at Coralie like a knife. It seemed to proclaim pride of possession to anyone interested enough to watch. Whatever Janice's motives, Coralie told herself that she could say goodbye to the cosy little lunch for two.

But Janice gently pushed Scarlett back into his chair. "Please, get on with your meal. If you're anything like me you must be famished!" She looked round for her companions. "I'm with Zelda and Anne-Marie. We've been given lunch here as a present for being good girls and working like dogs since daylight."

She looked at Coralie, her lovely green eyes wide, and then she giggled. "What do you think of my gear, Coralie? Dreadful, isn't it? But I have to show willing and wear it as an advertisement for the people who are paying me."

"What are you doing in Manchester?" asked Scarlett abruptly. "I thought you were in London."

Coralie thought he sounded put out, and wondered if it was because he hadn't been kept informed of Janice's whereabouts.

"Oh, we've been here for two days," she said carelessly, "working on a spring promotion for the Australian market. Their spring, that is, next September. Yesterday it was Salford with the busy industrial bit as background. Today it's been the Manchester Ship Canal—you know, the hoists and gantries and the whole dock-side scene, with the girls poised under a two-ton load being swung aboard." She laughed merrily. "What a way to earn a living! But I must go and eat," she said, looking across at her friends. "We're all ravenous." She joined the other two girls and immediately they fell into animated discussion of the menu.

Coralie hugged to herself the fact that Janice's left hand had been bare of rings, even though common-sense told her that a model would wear only the jewellery that the photographs demanded. Something else caught at her mind, something not quite in keeping with the behaviour of a newly-engaged couple. Surely Janice should have felt free to join Scarlett and herself if she had been his fiancée. Surely—

But there the fascinating train of thought was interrupted as Scarlett asked her to choose a dessert. "Janice is lovely, isn't she?" she asked as she ate her coffee meringue. He nodded tolerantly.

"Yes. Even in that weird outfit she looks good. What do you think of her for the catalogue?"

"Marvellous," Coralie said promptly. "Without the wig, that is."

He laughed. "Yes. I'm not sure if that would appeal to our customers."

Coralie watched Zelda and Anne Marie and wondered which was which. She thought Zelda would be the tall one with scraped-back blonde hair under a shapeless beret, and Anne Marie the brown-haired vivacious one. "They are three distinct types," she said thoughtfully. "Would they make a good combination for the catalogue?"

Scarlett could hardly weigh them up without turning right round in his chair, but he did so deliberately and quite blatantly. "Yes," he said, turning back. "You may be right there, and I feel the time is fast approaching when we must give someone a definite booking. I'll see what Janice thinks about it when I next see her."

Coffee arrived and she said impulsively, "Thank you for a lovely lunch, it was delicious. And thanks for bringing me over to Manchester."

He gave that now familiar little gesture with his hand, reminding her that he disliked being thanked.

"Should we be going?" he asked, looking at his watch.

"But—Janice hasn't finished," said Coralie. Surely he would want to spend a little time with her?

"I can't help that," he said. "We have a long drive home and it's almost three. I want to call in at the mill when I get back."

He went across to the other table, leaving Coralie puzzling once again why he had still been home at ten that morning. No wonder he needed to call at the mill. She saw him bend low to Janice and say something, then listen to her rapid reply with a hint of his captivating smile. Gaily Janice waved to Coralie and blew a kiss to Scarlett as they left.

Walking to the car Coralie found that the encounter with Janice had not dimmed her pleasure in the day's outing. It seemed that her decision to be grateful for whatever part of his life she could share had been a wise one.

Saturday evening found her standing in front of the mirror looking critically at her reflection and thinking rather wistfully how exciting it would be if she was all dressed up for an outing with Scarlett instead of Roger Greenfield. The memory of her one meeting with the younger man was fading rapidly, leaving only a vague picture of short-cropped blond curls and confident pale-blue eyes.

But she at any rate was looking her best. The silky sea-green dress showed off her creamy-gold skin, and she had taken back her wheat-coloured hair in soft loops and curls, threaded through with a string of silver beads which she had kept for years with her odd bits of jewellery.

She looked more slender than she had thought herself to be, and realised that she must have lost a few pounds in weight. The bias-cut material emphasised her slim hips and clung to her breasts in a way which she feared might look deliberately provocative, but there was no doubt that it suited her, and in fact could be mistaken for a very expensive model gown.

She quelled her misgivings with the thought that she could always keep the jacket on if she felt conspicuous, and in any case if Roger was prepared to drive sixty miles to pick her up and the same distance back again then he deserved a little glamour.

It was almost seven-thirty when the door-bell rang, but when she answered it she found Scarlett on the landing.

"Oh—come in," she said, stepping back hastily and sternly repressing a wild flutter of joy that for once he was seeing her looking her very best.

110

"We really must get you a phone installed," was his opening remark. Seeing her surprised expression he went on, "Then I wouldn't have to keep invading your privacy."

"Oh, but I don't mind," she said quickly. "That is—I realise a phone would make it more convenient for you, of course, and would save you the trouble of coming in person."

"It's no trouble," he said coolly, his stare taking in the dress from her bared shoulder down to the gracefully falling hem. "I'm thinking of my promise that you would be completely independent here."

His tone was perfectly courteous but Coralie detected a sardonic edge to it. What had happened to the easy friendship of yesterday?

"I have no complaints about lack of independence," she protested. "I love living here and I wouldn't want things any different."

If that sounded like a direct hint that his company was welcome it was just too bad, she thought uncomfortably. It certainly wasn't in line with her plan to be cool and distant, but she couldn't weigh up every single word before she uttered it.

"I see Roger is getting the full treatment," he said smoothly, his gaze on the dress once again.

So she hadn't imagined it. He was edgy! The faint colour rose in her cheeks, but some perverse impulse made her whirl round and say: "I made it during Easter, do you like it?"

"Yes," he said shortly. "You look very lovely. But I'm sure you have no wish to be delayed, so I won't keep you. I came across to see if you would like to come over to the house for tea tomorrow. My sister is coming for the day with her two little girls, and I thought it would be a change for you."

"I'd love to." She was pleased, and gave him her wide, spontaneous smile.

He was silent for a moment, while his gaze wandered slowly over her face and finally rested on her still-smiling lips. "Good. Come across any time during the afternoon. We'll be there. I don't need to wish you an enjoyable evening. I'm sure I can leave that in Roger's capable hands."

When he had gone Coralie stood behind the door pondering on his odd manner. Was he annoyed that she was going out with Roger? He had been too late with his own invitation, and she recalled that he hadn't been exactly pleasant on that occasion, either.

With a restless little shrug she turned away just as the bell rang again.

This time it was Roger, inches shorter than Scarlett, but every bit as broad, and with the resemblance to a young bull more pronounced than ever.

"Good to see you, Coralie," he said cheerfully, presenting her with a box of chocolates. "Austrian," he announced. "They're good. I've had some myself."

He looked her up and down as she thanked him. "You look terrific," he said seriously. When he came in he stared around with interest. "Pretty smart," he observed. "J.J. does you proud, doesn't he? I just passed him at the bottom of the stairs. How do you like living under the beady eye of the boss?"

"I don't mind," she said lightly. "And his eye isn't particularly beady."

"Let's go," said Roger. "I've booked a table for eight-thirty and I'm a bit late getting here. I thought we would eat at one place and then finish up at a club I know for a spot of dancing. Do you like to dance, Coralie?" Nimbly he executed a few rapid little steps, looking at her questioningly, and she couldn't help laughing. He was fun!

She picked up the jacket and he helped her into it, spreading a powerful aura of after-shave as he moved. "Hey, this is a nice outfit, Coralie," he said, deftly tying the neckband under her chin. "Your own work?"

"Yes," she admitted, and touched his wine-red dinner jacket. "Yours?"

"No, worse luck," he grinned. "It cost me a bomb in Paris. Let's go then, shall we?"

Once in the car he launched into tales of his exploits in some of the Common Market countries. He was an amusing man, quite witty, and with a childish delight in painting a picture of himself as an irresistible ladies' man. Coralie thought that his company would be entertaining for a few hours, but absolutely awful to live with.

They had been driving along dark, winding roads for a long time when he at last stopped the car in the courtyard of an inn. It was a big, rambling building built around an open yard, with low stone archways leading off in several directions, and in spite of its remote situation, it was full.

Roger proved to be an excellent host, knowledge-able about food and wine and attentive to a degree. True to his word he never once mentioned business, but kept the conversation on lighter topics throughout the long delicious meal. Looking around, Coralie was glad that she had taken trouble with her appearance. The other women were well-dressed, many of them very expensively, and when she removed her jacket in the warmth of the room she felt conscious of being the focus of a certain amount of attention, and not all of it feminine. Roger was staring at her and he shook his head admiringly. "You should show your shoulders all the time, Coralie. Your skin is like ripe, golden apricots."

She stiffled a giggle at his matter-of-fact tone. "I thought it was usually peaches and cream, not apricots."

He shrugged and wrinkled his broad flat nose. "I've no time for what's 'usual'," he said firmly. "I say what I like, and do what I like, and I get along fine."

"I'm sure you do," she said in amusement. "From

113

what you were telling me of the way you do business in Europe, no one could accuse you of bowing and scraping to obtain custom."

He laughed, the big dazzling teeth bared in what could be described as animal fashion if one wanted to be factual and ignore the strange, boyish charm of the man. "I find that people prefer it straight from the shoulder," he said. "They know I'm out for profit, so why wrap it up? Now—another coffee? A liqueur then? No? Surely you haven't finished already."

"Honestly Roger, that was a gorgeous meal. I couldn't eat another crumb or drink another drop."

"Well—if you're sure." He signalled for the bill and paid it with barely a glance. "Let's go," he said, and led her outside.

"This is a lovely place, Roger," she said as they went to the car. "It must be very old."

"Yes, it's on the old coaching route to Northumberland."

A fresh wind was blowing, bringing with it the cold peaty scent of the moors, and she felt the soft waves and tendrils of her hair escaping and blowing in confusion around her face. "Come here, Coralie," he said suddenly, taking her hand and side-stepping beneath a stone archway.

She went with him at once, expecting to be shown some interesting relic of bygone coaching days. But he took her firmly in his arms and kissed her thoroughly. There was little finesse about it. It was too brash, too sudden, too confident of an ecstatic reaction, and it was also quite impossible to escape. His lips were warm and not unpleasant, so for a moment she kissed him back; she was young, healthy, and she'd been kissed before. Then she remembered that she was dealing with a self-confessed expert on women, though his bull-in-a-china-shop approach made her doubt if his successes were as numerous as he made out. But enough was enough. She twisted her head away and

114

he released her, leaning back and smiling with a hint of satisfaction.

"That augurs well," he said appreciatively. "Come on, let's go and dance."

Augured well for what, she wondered. Their future relationship—or later that night? If the latter his long record of conquests was going to be broken, wasn't it?

But at the big country-club he said nothing to cause her concern, and he was certainly a marvellous dancer. He excelled in the Latin-American dances, and if she felt a trifle odd dancing the *paso-doble* in her elegant Grecian gown it was well worth it, because she thoroughly enjoyed herself as he spun her around with all the verve of a young matador with his cape.

His energy was inexhaustible, but once or twice she insisted on sitting out, and drank a fruit juice while Roger had brandy and soda. He drank sparingly, she was relieved to see. It would have been a disastrous end to the evening if he had been unfit to drive.

At one-thirty he asked if she would like to go home, and almost reluctantly she agreed. It was a rare pleasure in the age of discos and solo jigging to enjoy real ballroom dancing with an expert partner.

They set off for Raxby, and as the headlights swept ahead of them revealing the deserted road with moorland on either side she felt a twinge of uneasiness. If he was going to get amorous again this was the place he would choose.

But she was quite wrong. He had a more comfortable location in mind. "We're about half-way between Raxby and Leeds now," he said suddenly. "Is it to be your place or mine?"

"What?" she asked blankly.

"Your place or mine," he repeated. "Your flat in Raxby or mine in Leeds."

"For what?" she asked slowly, knowing what was coming.

"For the night. Oh, come on, Coralie. You know I fancy you. You're not going to send me off with just a kiss and a cuddle, are you?"

She knew she should have been furious but his approach was so open and somehow, so schoolboy-ish that she could only smile tolerantly.

"I don't go in for that sort of thing, Roger," she said firmly.

"What—never?" The incredulity in his voice was comical.

"No. Never."

"But I—" he broke off as someone overtook them, dangerously close. "Maniac!" he said placidly, gazing after the other driver. "That fellow was at the Club—I recognise the car." He looked at her sideways. "I thought you fancied me, too."

"I like you, Roger, but—"

"But—nothing doing, is that it? Oh well, it was worth a try. Time will tell."

With no visible change in his good humour he drove rapidly along the black roads, and, quite reassured at his placid acceptance of her refusal, she nodded sleepily at his side.

The harsh scream of brakes dragged her back to reality as the safety-belt dug into her chest. Roger fought with the car and brought it rapidly to a halt. "It's that maniac again," he roared, furious now. "He's crashed his car!"

The car that had overtaken them earlier was slewed across the narrow road, its hood up against a low stone wall. The man at the wheel seemed to be unhurt, sitting in the driving seat and rubbing his forehead wearily. Roger leapt from the car and went to him. There was the sound of raised voices, and then the sudden tinkle of glass. Coralie was about to follow him when he came back to her.

"He's all right," he said contemptuously. "But he needs a breakdown van. I've told him we'll send one out—there's an all-night garage when we reach the main road." He started the car, and then exclaimed in dismay, "I'm bleeding," he said, amazed, and she saw that his wrist was flowing with blood. "It must be from his headlamp. I was going to have a look at it but it fell apart. That's all we need," he said irritably. "I'll go back and bash his fat head in if I get blood on my new jacket."

Obviously he hadn't seen the dark splashes on her dress, and in spite of her dismay Coralie could almost have laughed as she pressed his handkerchief to his wrist. The similarity to a schoolboy was again apparent. A belligerent schoolboy this time, spoiling for a fight.

But the cut was deeper than they had thought, and it was a few minutes before they had bound it suitably with a makeshift bandage.

"What a blood-bath," he said, with a faint note of pride in his voice. "I shall have to give the car a good clean tomorrow."

"And I shall have to wash my dress," said Coralie, looking at it dolefully. "Come on, Roger, let's get back so that I can have a proper look at your hand."

She was glad that he seemed fit to drive. The idea of handling the sleek sports car on the winding roads until they reached civilization didn't appeal in the least.

It was another hour before they finally arrived at the flat, and she was hardly surprised when she saw it was three o'clock.

"Please be quiet," she begged. "I don't want to waken everyone."

He said, "I thought J.J. didn't keep his beady eye on you."

"He doesn't," she flashed. "I'm completely independent—I do what I like."

"That makes two of us," said Roger, a trifle wearily, she thought.

When she saw the makeshift dressing she told herself that it was no wonder he sounded tired.

It was soaked and clotted with blood, his trousers were a gory mess where more had dripped from his wrist, and his beautiful wine-red jacket was saturated and sticky.

"Oh, Roger!" Horrified, she rushed for the first-aid box. Remorse filled her for letting him drive, and mad thoughts whirled through her head. Should she ring the hospital? Did he need stitches?

But when she had cleaned it up they found that there was no real cause for alarm. It was certainly not the artery, but a deep cut at the base of the thumb.

Anxious to make up for what she now saw as her criminal stupidity in expecting him to drive in such a state, Coralie practically ran around the flat doing what was necessary to bandage his wrist and make him comfortable.

"You'll have to stay until morning," she said awkwardly. "You can't drive sixty miles and risk starting it bleeding again."

"I know," he said. "But don't worry, I'll be a good boy." He was pale, but his eyes still had that very cheeky glint, and she smiled back at him bleakly. With a bit of luck she could get him out of the way early in the morning before anyone was up and about.

"Take off your dress, Coralie," said Roger suddenly.

"What? Oh—yes. Yes, I will. I'll soak it in cold water and salt. That's what you should do with bloodstains, isn't it? Your trousers as well—are they washable? I'll bring you something else to put on."

He sat on the settee, draped modestly in a pink sheet, while she soaked the terylene trousers and sponged his jacket. She took off the dress and put on her towelling robe, then put the dress and jacket in the bath.

She was making a drink when she noticed that a light still shone from the window of Scarlett's study.

Hastily she drew the kitchen curtains, unwilling to let him, of all people, see that she was dressed in her bathrobe while Roger was in her flat.

She could barely keep awake as she brushed her hair before getting into bed. Roger was fast asleep covered by a spare blanket on the settee, and she had just put his trousers to dry on the bathroom radiator, having realised belatedly that he couldn't very well go home in the morning without them.

For a moment she thought about the light still burning in Scarlett's study. How could he lecture her about overworking when he drove himself even more relentlessly? She yawned widely as she got into bed. It had been a hectic evening—the long drives, the energetic dancing session, the incident with the other car.

At breakfast the next morning Roger was his usual bouncy self, bright-eyed and talkative, while Coralie felt so tense she found it difficult to swallow so much as a mouthful of food.

How could she have taken everything so calmly last night? In the harsh light of morning it seemed quite outrageous to be sharing breakfast with a man she hardly knew.

"What's up, Coralie?" asked Roger, ploughing his way energetically through a huge helping of cereal.

She looked at him, irritated. Was it her imagination or did he seem pleased with himself? Perhaps even a trifle smug? He was enjoying the fact that he'd stayed the night, wasn't he? Suddenly she knew that he would drive off with the maximum noise, car-doors slamming, exhaust roaring, just to let everyone know that he had made another conquest.

"If you must know, Roger, I don't care to be thought of as a girl who lets a man stay the night on their first date, when I hadn't the slightest intention of doing any such thing."

"Ha!" he pounced. "I knew it! You're worried about what J.J. will think, aren't you?" He looked away from her and asked casually, "Do you fancy him, then, Coralie? Is that it? He's a handsome fella, isn't he?"

Whatever his attributes, nobody was ever likely to say that about Roger. Handsome he was not. She wondered if beneath the bold exterior he was sensitive about his looks, and sought to reassure him.

"Fancy Mr. Scarlett," she repeated in a creditable show of amazement. "I certainly don't! I don't think he's particularly handsome, and—" she searched for a more convincing reason, "—he's too old. In any case, his interests lie elsewhere."

"Yes," agreed Roger quietly. "He plays the field, doesn't he? He gets all the beauties, does J.J. But everybody has despaired of him settling down. I think it's because of that awful business when he was running off with—what's-her-name—Melanie."

"Running off with her?" With an effort Coralie kept her voice steady. She saw that Roger's pale blue eyes were assessing her reactions, and knew that he hadn't believed her when she denied fancying Scarlett.

"Yes, you've heard something of it, I expect; J.J. was young, about twenty or so, and Melanie was an only child—doting parents, quite elderly, I think. They lived over the hills somewhere—Moss Fell, or somewhere in that direction. J.J. wanted to marry her, so the story goes, and the parents wouldn't agree because she was only seventeen and J.J. was still at university. So they decided to go off in secret and live together in order to force her parents into agreeing. They arranged to meet at their usual place up in the hills—a derelict farm I think it was—and go off together.

"But it started to snow and before long it was a positive blizzard. She didn't even reach the rendezvous and in the end he had to summon help to search for her. It was the next day before they found her—dead beneath a drift. Since then I don't recall

J.J. coming anywhere near marriage. It must have hit him hard."

"Yes, it must," she agreed steadily. "What a dreadful story." The trite little remark may have deceived Roger, for he made no further comment, but went on with his breakfast while she toyed with a piece of toast. There was something else she must clear up with him, she remembered.

"Roger, when you rang from Amsterdam you said something about me doing you a favour by persuading J.J. to include the lightweights."

"That's right. I remember."

"I just wanted you to know that it had nothing to do with you. I had almost forgotten your mentioning it to me."

He eyed her curiously. "So?"

"So nothing. I just didn't want you to have the wrong idea, that's all."

"I see. It wasn't the only wrong idea I had, was it?" He grinned in self-mockery. "What I like about you, Coralie, is—you're different. You're so different!"

Whether that was meant as a compliment she had no way of knowing. But time was getting on. Everyone across at the house would have been up and about ages ago.

"Are you sure your wrist will be all right when you drive?" she asked as he left the table, and he laughed mischievously.

"All right. I get the message. It's time I cleared off. Yes, it's okay, Coralie. No more signs of bleeding." He picked up the dinner jacket, "This has had it, I think," he said ruefully. "Well, thanks, Coralie—for a great evening and a good night's sleep. I'll be seeing quite a bit of you when we start production, but in the meantime what about another date?"

"A bit later on, perhaps, Roger. Leave it a week or two, will you?"

"Oh come on, cheer up, Coralie. It's not the end of the world to have a fella stay the night, you know." With a smile he kissed her cheek gently, and touched her chin with a short, stubby finger. At that moment, in spite of his words, he looked oddly unsure of himself, and rather ill-at-ease.

"I'm all right, Roger," she said reassuringly. "I'll be seeing you."

He ran lightly down the stairs, his jacket over his arm, and as she had known he would, slammed the door of the car.

A tall figure was coming towards the house as if returning from an early walk. Coralie watched tensely from the landing as Roger waved to her from the driving seat, and then turned and lifted his hand casually to Scarlett. He in turn nodded to Roger, who drove off with a flourish and disappeared from sight down the lane.

Uneasily, and feeling utterly brazen waving goodbye to a boy-friend at eight-thirty in the morning, Coralie looked down at Jethro Scarlett. She couldn't read the expressive eyes from where she stood at the top of the stairs, but his voice was unperturbed as he said quietly, "Good morning, Coralie."

"Good morning, Mr. Scarlett," she replied, and went indoors.

Eight

Coralie drove away from Raxby, obeying an impulse to leave everyone behind and find complete solitude in which to have a good think.

After a few miles she pulled off the road and stopped the car, but stayed behind the wheel staring out at the deserted landscape. A strong wind was blowing, bending the tough pliable grasses and combing them through with its force.

"Somewhere up in these hills is the derelict farm where Jethro arranged to meet Melanie," Coralie told herself painfully, ignoring the tears which stung her eyes as she thought of it. The whole affair seemed to be totally out of keeping with his character as she had read it. Even making allowance for his extreme youth at the time, it was surely very selfish to have persuaded a seventeen-year-old girl to leave a sheltered home in order to run off and live with him? And then to expect her to find her own way to a lonely rendezvous on a dark night, and in heavy snow?

Coralie could hardly believe that the man she loved had done those things. Against her will a feeling of distaste swept over her, replacing the horrified compassion she had felt before she knew the full story. There was an unpleasant air of bravado about it, a strange echo of Victorian melodrama, making the Scarlett of those earlier years appear in retrospect a wilful and very immature young man.

She looked up when the racing clouds obscured the sun, reducing the bright beauty of the moors to a sullen, menacing wilderness, and she wriggled restlessly in her seat. That night when she herself had been lost he had admitted loving Melanie, so how could she doubt that the tale was true?

Impatient with the misery which engulfed her at the memory of his unwavering admission she got out of the car, and immediately the wind tore at her hair, sending it streaming like a pale banner behind her.

She thought about the previous night, wondering if it would be best to try and forget it. There was really no necessity to make grovelling explanations and excuses. Scarlett was always harping on about her living independently, and was not averse himself to rolling home at five a.m. with a female in tow. She resolved not to mention Roger staying the night unless he did so first.

She sat on a low boulder and munched an apple thoughtfully. She realised that something had gone from her relationship with Scarlett—a little of her respect for his personal integrity had disappeared. A man who had done what he did to Melanie could never again be quite the same in Coralie's eyes. She thought of her parents, prevented from marrying for years, but waiting and waiting until at last they were free to build a wonderful marriage together.

But did it matter what she felt about him, she asked herself. It wasn't as if she had to make a big decision on whether to accept or reject a passionate proposal of marriage. She was merely his employee.

The daffodils on the curving grassy banks in front of Raxhead were nodding and bending before the wind when she drove into the courtyard. She could hear shrill childish voices, and round the corner of the house raced two little girls, dark-haired and chubby, wearing dungarees and warm sweaters.

They stopped, suddenly shy when they saw her,

then the older girl asked curiously, "Are you Coralie?"

"Why yes, I am. How did you guess?"

"Because I know you live in the coach-house!" said the child triumphantly. "I'm Emma, and I'm seven. This is Alexandra—she's five." She dragged the smaller child forward and together they stared at her with big blue eyes.

"What are you playing?" Coralie asked. "It sounded very exciting."

"Hide and seek," said Alexandra eagerly. "We've looked everywhere but we can't find him."

"Who are you searching for?"

"Uncle Jethro, of course," Emma shook her curly dark head reproachfully, as if Coralie was being very dense. "Will you help us to find him?"

The idea of searching for an unsuspecting Jethro Scarlett didn't much appeal to her. She wanted to find out how things were between them, to find out if she felt any differently towards him since hearing the story of Melanie, but not just yet. Not until she had finally sorted out her thoughts on the matter.

"Your eyes are shiny," observed Alexandra with devastating candour. "Have you been crying?"

"No, of course not," Coralie replied, "but you'd better carry on searching for him; he'll be getting tired of his hiding place."

With squeals of laughter they ran off, leaving Coralie looking after them, her tawny eyes still suspiciously shiny.

By the time she went across to the house for tea she felt more serene, having told herself quite firmly that what had happened years ago in Scarlett's life was none of her business; and just as clearly, what happened in *her* life—last night for instance—was no business of *his.* She would try to forget the Melanie affair, and revert, if she could, to a cool, friendly manner in her dealings with him.

He answered the door himself, and for a moment

their eyes met and held, but she found it impossible to fathom what lay behind the expressionless blue gaze. She took a deep breath, relieving the pain in her chest which was becoming a familiar sensation at each meeting with him.

"Ah, Coralie," he said cheerfully. "Come in. Two young ladies are waiting to talk you to death."

The drawing room doors opened and the little girls ran out. Alexandra caught hold of Coralie's hand. "I won't say anything about you crying," she said comfortingly. "Come and see my Mummy."

Scarlett shot a quick look at Coralie, "What does she mean?" he asked, his voice low.

"Oh, when we met this morning she wanted to know if I'd been crying," said Coralie awkwardly.

He stood before her, barring her entry to the room. "And had you?"

The time of sheer misery up on the moor came back to her, and against her will something of what she had felt then was mirrored in her eyes. But she managed a bright smile. "No, of course not."

He made no reply, merely looking at her closely as if waiting to judge for himself. Then he led her into the room.

"Helen, meet Coralie Dee. Coralie—my sister Helen."

They shook hands, each observing the other with interest. Helen was a younger, plumper version of her brother, with the same vivid blue eyes under long curving lashes.

"Hello, Coralie," she said warmly. "I believe my two chatterboxes have introduced themselves already. They've been excited for days about this visit, and I'm afraid they're a bit wound up. Come and sit by me so we can talk—if the girls will let us."

But Emma was already inching onto Coralie's lap with her favourite book and a rather bald koala bear, while her sister was close behind waiting to present Belinda, her doll, for inspection. Scarlett sat

126

by the window, watching them, his expression thoughtful. After a while the girls went back to monopolising him and there was opportunity for Coralie to get to know Helen. The older woman seemed a happy, uncomplicated person, deeply devoted to her husband and children, and with a warm, sensible way of dealing with her daughters which appealed to Coralie.

A sudden squeal of triumph indicated that Emma was winning at Snakes and Ladders. "They just adore Jethro," said Helen fondly, "and he's an absolute pet with them. I do wish—" she broke off and laughed apologetically. "I was going to say I wish he would find a nice girl and marry her, but I don't want you to think I'm trying to do a bit of match-making."

Coralie laughed, the colour warming her cheeks. "Of course I don't," she said quietly, "but I like to think that your brother and I are friends. He's been very kind to me since I came to Raxby, and he's certainly a very generous employer. He—" she kept her voice carefully casual—"he has no immediate plans for marriage, then?"

Helen looked at her, slightly puzzled, "Jethro? No, I'm sure he has nothing of that sort in mind at the moment."

Coralie bent her head to conceal the blaze of joy that consumed her. He wasn't engaged to Janice after all!

Helen said hesitantly, "I worry about him, you know, Coralie. I suppose that seems silly to you. He's such a self-sufficient man, and I know he has plenty of feminine company, but basically I think he's lonely up here in this great house with only the Braithwaites for company."

Coralie remembered the day after the plane crash, when she had watched him stride off over the moors in the pouring rain. "Yes," she said gently. "I think you may be right. But try not to worry. He strikes me as a man who knows what he wants from life."

"Yes—but suppose what he wants isn't available—what then?"

"I'm sure if he wanted to marry someone she would make herself available," said Coralie, more revealingly than she knew.

Helen started to reply, but changed her mind and kept silent, and at that moment, their game finished, Scarlett sent the girls off to ask if tea was nearly ready.

It proved to be an entertaining meal. Judith had made a children's tea, with tiny sandwiches, novelty cakes, jellies and ice-cream, and Scarlett was in high good humour—generating at full power was the way Coralie described it to herself.

Helen, too, seemed rather on edge, and once or twice Coralie caught her watching her brother with a vaguely puzzled frown.

He was charm itself when addressing Coralie, and she wondered why on earth she had even contemplated making detailed explanations to him about Roger. Quite obviously the fact that she had let him stay the night caused Scarlett not the slightest concern, and as Coralie tried to concentrate on Alexandra's chatter she suddenly realised why she felt in such low spirits.

She was disappointed! Fool that she was, she had been hoping he would be angry about it so that she would have an opening to explain. Even more important, his anger would have shown that he cared about what had happened!

All too soon it was time for Helen and the children to set off for home, and Coralie kissed them warmly when they proffered eager rosy cheeks. Scarlett submitted to hugs and squeezes galore, and returned the kisses blown energetically from the car as they set off.

It was a strange sensation to be standing at his side waving goodbye. This is what it would be like if I was his wife, she thought wistfully. Then we would go back into the house and shut the door on the outside world and—she collected herself guiltily. Was she quite mad—day-dreaming about being married to the man just because she was by his side on the porch? Hurriedly she said her farewells.

"Thanks for a lovely time, Jethro." She was shy now that they were alone. "They're beautiful children, aren't they?"

"Yes," he said seriously. "I'm very fond of them. Are you coming back indoors for a while?" He was as courteous as ever but it was by no means a pressing invitation.

With equal politeness she declined. "Thank you, no. I have a few things to do and then I must have an early night."

"I'm sure you're in need of it," he replied smoothly. "Good night, Coralie." And with that remark he turned and went into the house.

Liz came back full of vigour and vitality. She and Rob had spent their honeymoon in Ibiza, the first time either of them had been abroad, and she was full of the sights they had seen.

"You look terrible," she said bluntly to Coralie. "What on earth have you been doing to get those black circles under your eyes? Your mother will go mad if she sees you looking like that."

"Perhaps I've had a few too many late nights," admitted Coralie. "But I'm all right, really I am."

Soon the two girls were deep in discussion of the coming week's work, and, with the passing of the busy days, Coralie encouraged her personal life to recede as she was swept into the ever-increasing whirl of activity in the studio.

She saw Scarlett from time to time, but always in the company of other people; perhaps at a planning session for the catalogue, or when she showed some of her made-up designs to the working committee for their approval. He was quite pleasant and courteous, more so in fact than he had sometimes

129

been in the earlier days of their relationship, but she had learned to dread meeting the curiously blank stare of the once expressive eyes.

Did he, she wondered, feel that he had been too friendly with her, and that now he must put up the "keep-off" signs? He had often displayed an uncanny ability to read her thoughts—had he guessed how she felt about him? Such an attractive man, still unmarried, must have had to discourage women from time to time. He had probably found that a blast of that cold blue stare was enough to discourage anyone.

It hadn't taken Coralie long to realise that the business of Melanie had not changed her feelings towards him. She knew that something had been lost from her respect for him; but her day-to-day living was so filled with the longing to see him or hear him that she couldn't see a tall dark-haired man in the distance, or hear the phone ring, without that absurd leap of her heart and the painful sensation in her chest.

It was almost a relief to be with Roger again when she visited Greenfield's to examine the first samples to be made up before going into full production. She was impressed by the Greenfield establishment; well-equipped, well-designed, and with a seemingly enormous number of employees all busily sewing.

Roger, energetic and quick, showed her round, nodding his neatly-cropped head briskly when she congratulated him on the ultra-modern workrooms. "Good conditions and up-to-date equipment mean happy staff," he said. "We always expect the best work from our girls, and we usually get it."

They were back in his office by then, suddenly quiet with the door closed against the whirr of countless sewing machines. "Will you come out with me tonight, Coralie?" he asked, his voice loud in the stillness. "For a meal and then to the cinema or the theatre? Whatever you say. I promise to be a good boy." He waited for her answer with a quizzical lift of the blond eyebrows.

She smiled. "All right. How about a quick snack and then the cinema? It's ages since I saw a decent film."

She enjoyed the evening out, glad to lose the ever-present tension which overlaid her dealings with Scarlett. It was so different with Roger. He was so patently delighted by her company, so ready to listen attentively to her most casual remark, so light-hearted, so—so uncomplicated.

Yet she detected a subtle change in his manner towards her. Some of the boastfulness, the cocksure confidence, had gone; and in its place was a hesitancy, as if he wasn't quite sure how to treat her. Clearly her refusal of a few weeks earlier had given him something to think about.

They both laughed long and loud at the film. It was comedy with an off-beat type of humour which luckily appealed to them both. As they left the cinema she turned to Roger. "I really enjoyed that, Roger. I haven't laughed so much in ages."

He smiled as he started to drive her back to where she had left the Mini. "It's late," he said mischievously. "Are you sure you feel up to driving back to Raxby? My flat isn't far from here."

"Roger—" she said warningly.

"Okay, okay. So let me have just one tiny little kiss. That can't hurt, can it?"

He leaned across and planted a firm, warm kiss on her lips, then sat back in his seat, suddenly silent.

"Well—thanks for coming out with me, Coralie. Can I come up to see you in Raxby soon?"

"In a week or two, Roger. I still do a lot of work in the evenings."

He flared suddenly into anger. "J.J. has no right to expect it of you."

"He doesn't," she said at once. "He has told me, several times, to slow down a bit."

131

"Well, then, why don't you? You're entitled to some private life, surely?"

"Roger, please don't go on about it."

Coralie sighed and opened the car door. She had no intention of bickering about Scarlett. "Thanks again for a lovely time. Goodnight."

He stared at her, his aggressive eyes suddenly baffled, "But—oh well—be seeing you, Coralie. Cheerio."

It was late when she turned into the courtyard at Raxhead, her headlights spearing out to the dark moors behind the house. The inevitable light burned in Scarlett's study, and rather forlornly she stood for a moment staring at it, then, impatient with herself, she dashed up the stairs to her flat.

Once inside she felt tired but restless, and on impulse she put on the Sibelius symphony and played it quietly as she prepared for bed. It seemed an eternity since that night in his study when he had held her hands as she attempted to resign. What a lot of heartache she would have been spared if he had let her do it and she had gone back home to Somerset!

She sat on the rug in front of the fire and thought back to her various encounters with him. What he had said, how she had replied, the way in which he had looked at her. She shivered suddenly as she recalled the blank impersonal glance when he had met her in the weaving shed only that morning. Rather different from the time he had dragged her out and berated her about having her hair loose!

The last notes echoed on the air and she put the record away. It was high time she went to bed instead of indulging herself with utterly pointless recollections.

By the third week in May the pressure of work had eased somewhat, and Coralie was pleased that she would have a little more leisure during her mother's visit. She had been touched that both Liz and Miss Silverwood had issued invitations in advance of Francine's arrival, and had arranged to visit them both during her stay.

The weather had turned very warm, and one day when she went for lunch Coralie was delighted to find the big sliding windows of the dining hall open on to a long paved terrace where tables were set out under colourful umbrellas for anyone who wished to eat out of doors.

It was a bright summery scene, with the thronged terrace above the turbulent little river. Scarlett couldn't be faulted when it came to making things pleasant for the workers, Coralie thought, as she ate her excellent lunch.

She waved to Jim, her friend from the weaving shed, as he passed with a loaded tray to join his workmates. Just then a group of girls close to Coralie stopped their chattering and fell silent. One of them giggled and whispered excitedly to her friends. Idly, Coralie looked up to see what was affecting them. It was Scarlett, weaving his way between the tables. He stopped from time to time to have a word with someone, but it soon became evident that he was aiming for Coralie.

Her heart began its usual cavorting, and she forced herself to breathe normally. He stopped by her table and said, "May I join you for a moment?"

"Of course. Please do."

The idiotic thought flashed through her mind that were it not for her smock and Scarlett's business suit they might almost have been a couple on holiday at some continental hotel, with the sun shining from a cloudless sky and the last tawny blooms of the wallflowers making a brave show above the water. She waited expectantly to see what he wanted.

"Sorry to interrupt your lunch," he said, not sounding in the least repentant. "I called in at the studio hoping to catch you before you came down, but I was too late. Can you type, by any chance, Coralie?"

"Why—yes. Not very fast, but fairly accurately."

"Sylvie's gone home sick with a sore throat and temperature. I had to practically order her off the premises because we were working all-out on the French contracts—filling in a lot of complicated facts and figures. I could get a girl from the typing pool, but none of them is fluent in French, and although I can get along quite well verbally I have to admit that typing the French language isn't one of my accomplishments. I wonder—could you spare the afternoon to come along to my office and help me out?"

"Why, of course!" She beamed at him, pleasure flooding through her because he needed her help. "Shall I come now?"

"Steady, steady. Not so fast. Finish your lunch break, and if you could come along about two, or as soon after that as you can."

At once he rose to go, and without thinking she started to ask if he himself had eaten. "Have you—?" She stopped abruptly, telling herself that he wasn't a teenage boy to be questioned about his intake of food.

"Have I what?" he asked curiously.

"I just wondered if you've had your own lunch, that's all," she said, feeling a fool.

The merest hint of the brilliant smile touched his lips. "I'm not likely to starve, I assure you, Coralie. I have a snack sent up to the office. I prefer it. It's quiet with everyone out of the way and the phones disconnected, and I can work in peace."

"I don't see how you can tell me off for working too hard," she said at that. "You're much worse than I am."

"As your employer I feel responsible for your well-being," he replied soberly. "What I do with my time is my own concern. I'll see you at two."

"Consider yourself put firmly in your place, my girl," said Coralie to herself as he walked away. She finished her coffee, deep in thought. Seen at such close quarters across the little table he had looked tired—if such a description could ever be applied to so energetic a man. She fancied that there had been a weary line to the firm lips, a heaviness to the dark-lashed eyelids. And no wonder. His social life seemed more hectic than ever, because several times a week she heard him return to Raxhead in the small hours and even when he was at home he stayed up late in the study. Now he calmly informed her that he liked a quiet lunch break in order to work!

Uneasily she looked down at the tumbling waters of the river. What on earth was driving the man?

When she went to the cloakroom to tidy herself up before going to his office, she was glad that she had taken to wearing something decent under her smocks. The warm weather had tempted her to put on a sleeveless voile dress which hung loosely from a latticed yoke. It was a filmy, airy creation of her own in a deep cream colour which made her tawny eyes look darker, and showed off the first faint bloom of the tan which she had acquired during a day at the coast the previous weekend.

When Liz came back from lunch she opened her eyes wide. "You look gorgeous," she said. "Super dress—it suits you."

"I'm going off for a while to help J.J. with a French contract," explained Coralie. "Miss Silverwood has gone home ill. Do you want to ask me anything before I go?"

Together they discussed the evening dress which Liz was sewing, and then Coralie left the studio for Scarlett's office, her heart thudding uncomfortably at the prospect of being alone with him for the first time in weeks.

It was evident that no such misgivings troubled her employer. Brisk, business-like, and with the blank blue stare in frequent use, he was pleasantly polite but no more. "Perhaps you'd like to give me your opinion on these, before we begin," he said, handing her a sheaf of glossy coloured photographs. "They're the prints I told you about—sent for our approval by the agency who employ Janice and Zelda."

Intently Coralie examined the photographs, which she knew had been commissioned solely to see if the two models "came over" as the right types for the catalogue. The vivacious Anne-Marie had been unavailable, being booked for months ahead, but both Janice and Zelda had a few free days in their schedules.

Critically Coralie eyed the pictures and felt a stirring of pride in her work. The clothes looked terrific now that they were shown off on live models, and Janice in particular looked lovely. Zelda, tall and almost bony, lent her own gauntly elegant air to the classic winter coats she modelled.

"They both look marvellous," she said enthusiastically.

"Mm," he said non-committally. "The agency have offered us another model, a more mature woman. We'll have a few pictures of her by the weekend. I was wondering if it might be a good idea to include an older woman, what do you think?"

"Yes—if she's the right type," agreed Coralie cautiously. "After all, many of the designs are meant to appeal to several age groups. How silly of me not to have thought of having an older model."

He neither agreed nor disagreed, merely remarking, "We'll leave any decisions until we see how she looks in the clothes. Now, let's get on, shall we?"

Within minutes they were involved in a series of measurements, prices, and technical descriptions of the cloth, to be used in a pilot scheme being prepared by a French ready-to-wear house. It was hoped the inital order would lead to regular custom from them in the future.

Painstakingly they worked their way through his

notes, Coralie translating as she took down the details at his dictation. After a while he said, "Sylvie usually sits this side of the desk when we're working on something as intricate as this. It's easier if we want to check each other's figures. Come round here, Coralie."

Picking up a chair he put it next to his own, and she walked slowly round the desk, trying hard not to appear reluctant.

He watched her and exclaimed irritably, "Good grief, girl, don't look so petrified. I'm not going to eat you!"

Swallowing the sharp retort that sprang to her lips she sat down next to him and proceeded to pencil in a list of metric lengths, maintaining what she hoped was a dignified silence. After a moment she sensed that he was watching her, and she looked up quickly, surprising a strange expression in his eyes. It was a deep, painful sadness. Almost—she thought in astonishment—almost a kind of despair.

Obeying an impulse so strong it defied all reason and logic she put out her hand and touched his. "What is it?" she asked quietly. "What's wrong? Why are you so sad—and—so angry? You said once that we were friends—is there anything I can do to help?"

It was, in effect, her olive branch, her peace offering, made out of compassion for the sorrow she had glimpsed in that unguarded moment, and also out of her own need to end the hollow nothingness of their present relationship.

Conscious that she had far outstepped her role of dutiful employee, she stared down at the stiff, unmoving hand beneath her own. At his prolonged silence she raised worried amber eyes to his, and recoiled at the open hostility she saw there.

"I am not sad," he said clearly and deliberately. "Neither am I angry. But even if I were, what makes you imagine that it is any business of yours?"

137

It was the most deliberate snub of Coralie's life, spoken intimidatingly and with cruel clarity. The blood rushed to her cheeks and she released his hand as if it was red-hot. To her horror she felt tears of humiliation sting her eyelids. She bent her head and blinked rapidly. "I beg your pardon," she said quietly. "It was not my intention to pry."

There was a silence, during which he bent over his papers with every appearance of concentration. Coralie watched him and felt cold fury building up inside her. He was lying when he said that he was neither sad nor angry. She wasn't an idiot. She had seen the expression in his eyes just then, and she could hardly have failed to notice his ill-humour.

And then, quite suddenly, a horrifying thought hit her like a blow. It was her work! He was disappointed in it! All these weeks he had been waiting for an improvement, hoping that his choice of her as designer would be proved right. She had made a good beginning and he had complimented her on it, and like a complacent fool she had gone on producing designs which he must have found inferior.

She jumped to her feet and dumped her notes on his desk. "It's my designs, isn't it?" she demanded tensely. "You don't like them but you couldn't bring yourself to tell me! I've gone on and on working like a mad thing and all the time you knew my work was no good!"

He rose to his feet as well, astonishment at her outburst mingled with a kind of shocked dismay on his face. "What on earth are you talking about?" he asked, his deep voice so low it was almost a growl.

"You know very well!" she accused passionately. "You've been absolutely horrible for weeks and weeks—you, who gave me all that stuff about creative people needing to be happy and contented."

"And aren't you?" he asked slowly.

"N-no. Of course I'm not!" She pushed her hair back and looked up at him defiantly.

"Because I've been 'absolutely horrible'?" She thought the disbelieving tone held just a hint of ridicule. Put like that it made her sound neurotic, and she pushed out her lips mutinously, ignoring his question.

"Am I right?" she persisted, her voice still unsteady. "Is it my work?"

"Your work is brilliant, imaginative, painstaking, and a constant delight to me," he said calmly. "And that is not overstating how I feel about it."

"Oh." She stared at him, at a loss what to say next. But he hadn't finished.

"If I had not been satisfied with it you can rest assured that I would have managed to summon the courage to tell you so. You're overwrought, you're more than a little tired, and so you're imagining things. If I have been 'horrible' as you put it, I apologise. I should have been more considerate of your feelings."

She sighed. Already she was regretting her impulsive words, and wondering what she might inadvertently have revealed. He was, after all, extremely perceptive. Even so, he had been surprised into stating an obviously genuine opinion of her work, and it had both delighted and encouraged her.

"Please," she said quietly, "don't apologise. You're quite right. I was a little overwrought and said several foolish things. Now, should I start typing the contract?"

"If you're quite sure you feel up to it," he said, and looking far from energetic himself he went to open the door to Miss Silverwood's room.

Nine

Coralie visited Miss Silverwood at home, taking
flowers and magazines and some home-made deli-
cacies from Judith. She found the invalid restive,
obviously reluctant to be away from her job, and
filled with misgivings about her employer being at
the mercy of a girl from the typing pool. Privately
Coralie thought it was more a case of the girl from
the typing pool being at the mercy of Scarlett, but
she refrained from saying so.

Miss Silverwood had left Coralie in no doubt of
her gratitude for the way she had helped out with
the French contract; but Coralie recalled that Scarlett himself had hardly been effusive when she
presented him with the typed contract and the
specification, with its tables of complicated figures
and measurements all scrupulously checked.

He had looked them over briefly, and glanced
keenly at her flushed face, saying soberly, "Thank
you, Coralie. I appreciate your help, especially as it
was so willingly given."

It was enough. She had been able to help him
when he needed it. She forgave him on the instant
for the humiliating snub, and bestowed on him her
wide, truly beautiful smile. Then she walked back
slowly along the deserted corridor.

She saw little of him after that until on Friday
afternoon he called at the studio with photographs
of the third model, and together they agreed they
would be unlikely to better the attractive grey-

haired woman. Scarlett, unlike his usual energetic self, lingered aimlessly, and was staring out of the window when the door opened and Roger breezed in.

"Hi, Coralie—oh, hello J.J. I thought I'd better come over to sort out the skirts of those light-weight suits. My man tells me that the pleats aren't holding too well in that particular cloth. I've brought a couple of examples over with me."

Coralie knew that he could quite easily have let someone else deal with the problem, and she realised that he must have seized on the excuse to come to Raxby in person. He had rung her several times since their outing to the cinema, and each time she had put him off as tactfully as possible.

Scarlett might almost have had similar doubts about the necessity for the visit, judging by his somewhat sceptical expression. But Roger, outwardly as cocksure as ever, launched into technical details and in a moment they were all deep in discussion, with the whirr of Liz's machine to be heard all the while from the room next door.

At last Scarlett left, and to Coralie's dismay Roger hardly waited for the door to close behind him before saying: "Good. I thought he'd never go and leave us alone. How about a kiss?"

Before she could think of a suitably crushing reply Roger pulled her in to his beefy embrace and kissed her very thoroughly.

Even as she struggled to push him away Coralie sensed the presence of Scarlett back in the room. She twisted round to face the door, Roger still holding her, and to her horror saw that her employer was in fact in the doorway. She stared at him with shocked, embarrassed eyes, part of her mind registering that Roger was deliberately pressing her against his chest.

She heard the deep voice saying in level, dispassionate tones: "It seems I've returned with inconvenient speed, but since I'm here I may as well make one thing clear to you both. However intimate your relationship may be elsewhere I would prefer you to save your kissing and cuddling until after working hours, when you are off my premises."

Anger blazed in his eyes as Coralie finally wriggled free from Roger's grasp and stood by his side, facing Scarlett.

"Oh, come on J.J." Roger laughed. "It's quite a while since Coralie and I saw each other. You know how it is." The implication was there that they hadn't been able to wait to leap into each other's arms, and once again Coralie was certain that Roger was enjoying himself hugely.

She swallowed, her mouth suddenly dry, and opened her lips to protest. But Scarlett forestalled her. "Yes. I do know how it is—with you, Greenfield. I gave Coralie credit for a little more discretion." He looked at them both for several seconds, his eyes steady and filled with a cold distaste. Then he left the room.

"Roger! How could you!" Coralie burst out, driven to fury by the pleased expression on his fair features. "You're impossible. You—oh, you make me sick! Please go. I have work to do."

"So—" he said slowly. "I was right. You fancy him, don't you? I thought as much." For an instant raw jealousy showed behind the pale, confident eyes, followed by a shrewd, calculating assessment of the situation. She glared at him speechlessly.

"All right, all right. Keep calm. I'm going. But I'll be in touch. Oh yes, I'll be in touch. We still have an awful lot of business to discuss, don't forget."

When he had gone Coralie leaned weakly against the workbench, looking out at the brilliant sunshine. She felt quite ill as she re-lived the moment when Scarlett stood there watching her in Roger's arms. Was there to be no end to the misunderstandings between them?

"I couldn't help hearing most of that, Coralie." It

142

was Liz standing by her side, her puggy little face concerned and sympathetic.

"Oh Liz. Wasn't it awful?"

"J.J. didn't sound too pleased," Liz remarked thoughtfully. "And as for the bright boy—he seemed a bit put-out as well when you sent him packing."

"I know. He's—well to be frank, he's a bit persistent, Liz, and I have to keep giving him the brush-off."

Liz opened her eyes wide. "Our Mr. Roger isn't used to that. Oh no! He won't like that at all. The girls usually fall over themselves when he's around."

"Not this girl," said Coralie drily. "He's good company, but that's all. We've had two dates, and I certainly don't intend to let myself in for a third one after this afternoon." Words failed her, and she looked away, knowing she was on the verge of tears.

"Well, from what I heard, Roger waited until J.J. was out of the room," Liz pointed out reasonably. "He couldn't have known he would come back."

"No. I realise that. But it's typical of Roger. He's tried his cave-man tactics before."

The other girl stood there, attentive, friendly and sensible. For a moment Coralie was strongly tempted to confide in her, to pour out all the agonies and uncertainties of the last two months, but she couldn't bring herself to do it. What she felt for Jethro was too personal, too precious, to share with Liz, fond of her though she was.

"You could explain to Mr. Scarlett that it wasn't any of your doing—that Roger just grabbed you," suggested Liz. "That might pacify him."

"Pacify him!" Coralie cried. "If he chooses to jump to wrong conclusions and not give me a chance to open my mouth, then I'm not going to go grovelling to him with explanations in the hope of pacifying him! I'll leave it as it stands and he can think what he likes."

Liz kept silent, watching her with troubled, speculative eyes. After a moment she went back to her work, leaving Coralie staring out at the great rising curves of the moor. Her fury with Roger was abating rapidly and being replaced by a deep resentment against Scarlett. How could he just take it for granted that she was as eager as Roger to "kiss and cuddle" as he so charmingly put it?

Quickly she cut into a length of the printed polyester; and then she paused, laying down the shears. Be fair, she cautioned herself wearily. You only had to see him and Janice leaving a jeweller's shop to leap to the conclusion that they were engaged, quite wrongly as it happens.

But Scarlett knows that Roger spent the night with you. He probably also knows that you've had at least one date with him in Leeds, and that he telephones you frequently. Today he saw you both in a passionate clinch—what is he likely to think other than that you were as keen as Roger?

Coralie perched on the edge of the workbench, her sense of fair play appeased by such rational reasoning, but not feeling any the more cheerful for it. What had happened to the serene optimism of the days before she came to Raxby? Where was the carefree, sunny-natured girl who had sailed through her three-year design course? Gone for ever, by the look of it. Nowadays life was one long round of wondering if she would see him; worrying about what he was thinking if she did see him, and trying to imagine what he would say the next time she saw him!

It was ridiculous. She would have been more settled if he had become engaged to Janice. At least she would have known where she stood, and been able to plan some sort of life for herself, a life which didn't revolve around him every minute of the day!

But she would have to put her personal problems in the background for a while. Her mother was due to arrive at Raxby station at 6:30, and the next week must be devoted to making her visit enjoyable. Determinedly, Coralie picked up her shears again.

Francine was delighted with the flat. "It is beautiful, *chérie*. Yes, I know you told me, but I did not expect it to be so—so luxurious!"

They had just finished dinner that evening, a special meal planned and cooked with great care by Coralie, and now they were sitting with their coffee in front of the big picture window overlooking the valley.

The two of them had talked almost non-stop since Francine first stepped from the train, but they were still not up-to-date with each other's news.

"Your Mr. Scarlett—what sort of man is he?" asked Francine curiously. "You say little about him in your letters. Do you not like him?"

Coralie raised clear amber eyes to her mother's dark ones, knowing of old that she was impossible to deceive. "First of all he's not my Mr. Scarlett! As for the sort of man he is. . . . Impressive, as I told you after my interview, and at times incredibly kind. At other times he's bossy and horrible. Very energetic, very capable, and—yes, I quite like him."

Francine smiled slightly. "Perhaps I will meet him during my visit. He is certainly a generous employer." Her bright eyes rested momentarily on her daughter's face, then, with the sensitivity to her daughter's feelings which Coralie knew and loved, she left the subject. "Is that the mill I see down in the valley?" she asked.

"Yes, that's Scarlett's." Coralie stood at her mother's side, looking down on Raxby. The pale walls of the mill were lit by the rosy hues of sunset, and they could see the flag flying above the square corner-tower. The air was so clear that Coralie imagined she could see the big red S on it, and the twist of scarlet thread that was the Scarlett trade mark.

And then the valley became dark as the sun

slipped away behind a shoulder of the moor, leaving the sky still luminous above the lonely heights.

"Would you like to go down tomorrow to see the studio, *Maman?* I could take you over the mill as well, if you like."

"But of course I would. Will Mr. Scarlett not object?"

"Oh! Well—I suppose I should ask him first." Coralie tried valiantly to conceal her reluctance to do any such thing. How could she possibly face him after that awful scene?

But Francine was looking at her expectantly, so she said recklessly, "I'll just slip down and have a word with him while you unpack, if you like."

She found him looking serious and rather distinguished in immaculate evening dress, and about to set off somewhere in the two-seater. He glanced up from the driving seat as she hurried across the courtyard, and to her surprise he immediately got out and stood waiting for her, one hand outstretched against the low roof of the car.

"Please—you shouldn't have got out," she said breathlessly. "I won't keep you a moment. I just wanted to ask you if I could show my mother round the studio and the rest of the mill tomorrow?"

"Your mother?" he asked with interest. "Is she here?"

"Yes, she arrived this evening. She's staying with me for a week."

"Of course you may take her round the mill," he said, sounding a trifle perplexed. "You needn't have bothered to ask."

"Oh. Thanks." For a moment she looked up at him, dark-skinned and raven-haired when seen like that against the evening sky. She felt the strongest reluctance to turn away and leave him, which was crazy considering the unpleasantness of their last meeting a few hours earlier.

She was astounded to find him so pleasant after his earlier display of cold fury, and she found herself saying urgently, "Mr Scarlett—about this afternoon—it wasn't what you thought when you saw me with Roger. What happened was—it was without my agreement."

He looked at her consideringly, and then his firm lips softened slightly and he ran a hand through the thick hair. To her relief, he nodded. "When I gave thought to it I realised that you were very unlikely to have agreed to such a—" he paused, "such a display of affection, with Liz in the next room, and only seconds after I had left. It seems I owe you an apology. I'm sorry, Coralie."

"It's all right, Mr. Scarlett. I realise it must have looked awful at the time." Her mind raced madly. It hadn't taken him long to correct his own mistaken conclusions. Should she, perhaps, seize the opportunity and clear up any other wrong ideas he might have formed? She hovered uncertainly in front of him, trying to decide.

Meanwhile he looked down at her with a disturbed expression. "Coralie, I haven't forgotten that you told me you aren't happy at present. I hope I reassured you about your work, but I feel I must ask if I am the cause of your unhappiness. You made it clear to me that you thought I had been 'absolutely horrible.' Could you explain what you meant by that?"

She stared at him, transfixed. This was asking her to put her cards on the table with a vengeance. How could she say: "I'm unhappy because you look at me with blank, empty eyes; because you're angry with me and I don't know why; because you don't seem to care about my welfare the way you once did; because you're not bothered about Roger spending the night with me; because I believe you love Janice; and because, in addition to all that, I can't forget that you were mainly responsible for Melanie's death?"

So many reasons, but not a single one that she could explain to him. She tried, though, to give him

147

an edited version, phrasing it in carefully unemotional terms. "I have been rather unhappy at times, and for various reasons. And—yes—one of them was that I thought I had offended you, but I didn't know how, and I didn't feel I could ask. That's why I leapt to the conclusion that my work wasn't satisfactory."

"Did I say something to make you think I was offended?" he persisted, "I mean before that day when we worked on the French contract. Was I 'absolutely horrible' in any particular way?"

If she had been dealing with anyone other than the self-assured Jethro Scarlett, thought Coralie, she would have sworn that her childish phrase must have hurt him deeply. "It was just an impression I got," she said evasively. "You were quite pleasant and—and everything. I'm sorry—I can see that I shouldn't have said it. I think I told you at the time that I was a little overwrought."

"Mm. As we're having a grand apologising session, I want to tell you that I'm truly sorry for my unpardonable rudeness on that occasion. I think perhaps we were both rather on edge. Shall we make a fresh start, Coralie? I can't have you unhappy. Those great big golden eyes were made for laughter, not for tears. Are we friends again?"

"Friends," she agreed.

His lean brown hand took hers and enclosed it, releasing it only a second later as if the contact disturbed him. "I'd like to meet your mother before I go tomorrow. Could I call in to see her during the morning?"

"Go?" repeated Coralie, seizing on that one point.

"Yes," he said, sounding surprised. "I'm off to Denmark for a few days, didn't you know? There's been some sort of trouble with the firm who import our cloth over there. The Board have asked me to go to Copenhagen in person to see what I can do to pour oil on troubled waters."

She felt ridiculously bereft. He was going away

just as they had reached the verge of a better understanding. She collected herself. "No, I didn't know. But please come over to meet mother and have a coffee with us, Mr. Scarlett."

He raised one eyebrow.

"Oh—sorry." She cleared her throat. "Jethro."

With a flash of the brilliant smile he opened the car door and slid into the driving seat. "I'll see you tomorrow then, Coralie. Goodnight." And with a roar of the car's powerful engine he swept away down the hill.

From the moment next morning when Scarlett somewhat surprisingly kissed Francine's hand, Coralie could see that he was generating his considerable charm at full power. Evidently he liked her mother, and Francine in her turn seemed captivated by him.

But there were qualities in the fragile little woman which were not easily overpowered, even by so strong a personality as his. When Scarlett mentioned that he was delighted with Coralie's work, Francine looked him straight in the eye, and to Coralie's discomfort said calmly: "I can tell by the way my daughter has lost weight that she has been working very hard since coming to Raxby, and in all probability has not been getting enough rest. But that is understandable—I am sure she is intent upon making a success of her first appointment as a designer."

It was said with her customary exquisite courtesy, but it made plain her opinion that despite Coralie's salary, the lovely flat and the company car, honours between her and her employer were even. Scarlett nodded in agreement and said mildly, "She has impressed all of us at the mill with her enthusiasm, Mrs. Dee. We consider ourselves lucky to have her."

Not surprisingly, Coralie was restless at being discussed as if she was invisible, and hastily intervened to offer more coffee and shortbread. After that the conversation turned to Paris, Francine finding with pleasure that Scarlett knew the city extremely well.

With a tightening of the heart Coralie watched him rise to take his leave, but at that moment a florist's van drew up in front of the coach-house and a youth ran up the stairs carrying a great bouquet of mixed flowers.

"Those must be for you, *chérie*," said Francine with surprised pleasure, and Coralie went to the door.

"But *Maman*, they're addressed to *Mrs.* Dee," she said, coming back into the room. With a little laugh at the astonishment on her mother's face, she handed over the flowers.

Francine withdrew the card from its envelope and read it aloud. "'Hoping your stay in Raxby is an enjoyable one—Roger Greenfield.' But how kind! He is the young man you told me about, is he not, Coralie? The man from Leeds?"

"Yes," agreed Coralie shortly. "That's Roger. I mentioned to him the other day that you were coming." She shot a glance at Scarlett, but he was watching Francine, his expression unreadable.

Francine was sensitive to the change in the atmosphere. She laid the flowers carefully aside and said to Scarlett: "But our chatter is delaying your departure, and I'm sure you must be keeping to a strict timetable in order to catch your plane. It has been a pleasure to meet you, Mr. Scarlett."

He bowed slightly. "A mutual pleasure, Mrs. Dee." For a moment the old smile lit his features, and then he and Francine looked steadily at each other. Coralie gained the odd impression that each had sized up the other and drawn their own conclusions.

She went to the door with him. There was so much she would have liked to say, but in the end she merely said quietly, "Have a good trip, Jethro—and come back safely."

He stayed on the landing, the breeze ruffling his hair. "I hope to be back by next weekend at the latest. Will you keep Saturday evening free for me, and we'll go out to dinner—or will you still be entertaining your mother?"

"No, she goes home on Friday morning, because she's due back at the shop on Saturday. And of course I'll keep Saturday free for you." She smiled up at him.

He looked down on her, the startlingly blue eyes intent and for some reason rather puzzled. "Until Saturday then," he said abruptly, and went quickly down the stairs.

She told Francine that Scarlett was taking her out when he returned from Copenhagen, and her mother eyed her flushed cheeks with bright, observant eyes. "What will you wear?" she asked.

Coralie gave her a suitably edited version of her outing with Roger. "The dress and jacket are in the wardrobe," she concluded, "but I couldn't get the stains out. They're ruined."

"I will help you make another one," offered Francine at once. "We can do it easily in the time. Perhaps we could look for material on Monday when we go to the seaside."

"I'll see what material is available before deciding on the style," agreed Coralie. Already she had decided that the dress would be as different as she could make it from the sea-green polyester with all its unpleasant associations.

In the end she chose a satinized cotton in abstract swirls of deep gold and pink. "I like it," declared Francine. "It looks rather exotic, but it will be cool and comfortable. Have you decided on the style?"

"Sleeveless," said Coralie promptly, "with a scooped-out neckline, I think, or maybe backless with a halter-top, and a full, swirly skirt."

"You have a glorious tan," said Francine fondly. "Why not show it off?"

They spent the afternoon at a small deserted

beach. Coralie sitting in her brief black bikini with her sketching pad on her knees, working out details of the dress, and Francine relaxing with a novel.

The rest of the week sped past all too quickly, filled as it was with visits, outings and picnics. Each morning Coralie left Francine still in bed and went down early to the studio, so that she could take the afternoons off with a clear conscience.

One evening they had a meal with Miss Silverwood, now quite well again, and Coralie watched with interest as the plump, placid secretary chatted to the small, dynamic Frenchwoman. An attraction of opposites, perhaps, but they got on well together. In fact, Coralie was amused to see that Francine charmed everyone she met—Liz and Rob, Judith and Walter, and finally Roger.

He descended on them at the flat on Francine's last afternoon, after a one-sided telephone conversation with Coralie, during which he did all the talking and arranging without giving her the chance to get a word in.

He arrived driving a big white Rover, and wearing jeans with a checked shirt, casual gear which didn't flatter his stocky figure as much as the beautiful suits in which she had previously seen him.

His manner with Coralie was correct almost to the point of deference, making her wonder if he regretted his impetuous behaviour at their last meeting. With her mother he was, oddly enough, more relaxed; still cocksure it was true, but with all his usual boyish high spirits in evidence.

Francine, in her turn, was charming to the young man who had taken the trouble to send her flowers, and called him "Rogaire" from the start.

He took them out to tea at a lonely inn high on the moors north-west of Raxby, where they sat in a stone-walled garden and ate a prodigious high tea of cooked meats, salads, home-baked bread and cakes.

It was brilliantly sunny, with a soft breeze rippling the strong tufted grasses and sending the high white clouds in stately procession across the immense expanse of sky. In such lovely weather the little inn was a tranquil place, the quietness intensified by the clear impassioned song of a lark high above the garden.

Not for the first time Coralie acknowledged to herself that Roger could be very good company. His easy good-humour, his obvious pleasure in being with them, even his endless supply of funny stories all added to her enjoyment. She knew that Francine's presence would effectively prevent any of his bull-in-a-china-shop tactics, and that gave a final touch of relaxation to the afternoon.

Back at the flat they had a quiet supper, and as the bright day faded Roger suggested a walk across the hillside. As perhaps he had expected, Francine declined. "Not for me, Rogaire," she said quickly. "After so much fresh air I am sleepy. I will have a bath and then an early night to prepare for my journey tomorrow. You take Coralie for a little walk."

Coralie would have liked to refuse, but Roger had been so good, putting himself out to be nice to her mother, taking them to the remote little inn which they would never have found for themselves. She heard herself agreeing. "Just a short stroll, Roger. Like *Maman*, I'm a bit tired."

He shook hands with Francine. "Have a good journey, Mrs. Dee. I think we'll meet again before long."

If Francine considered that an unlikely prophecy, she gave no sign, but smiled warmly as she thanked him for their outing and said goodbye.

At once Roger took Coralie's arm in his powerful grip and led her off along the track past Raxhead. He was unusually silent, so much so that Coralie realised he had something on his mind and was reluctant to voice it. At last they reached a long low outcrop of rock where he sat down and looked up at her expectantly. "Sit down, Coralie."

She did so, leaving a good three feet between

them, and, seeing that, he laughed ruefully. "It's all right, I'll behave myself. I want to ask you something."

Then she saw his face. Eager, intense, and incredibly for Roger, bashful.

"Will you marry me?" he asked quickly.

She gaped at him, only with difficulty preventing her jaw from dropping.

"Yes, I know," he said rapidly. "It's a bit of a surprise to me, too, finding myself proposing to you."

"But Roger, you don't know me all that well, and—and I never thought marriage entered your scheme of things, anyway."

"It didn't—until I met you," he said simply. "I liked a good time with the girls and I picked them up and dropped them just as quickly. And when I met you I thought I could do the same. But as I've told you before—you're different, Coralie. I can't get you out of my mind."

"Are you sure it's not just because I won't jump into bed with you?" she asked bluntly. "For centuries men have proposed marriage for that very reason."

"I've thought of that," he said doggedly. "And yes—that's part of it, I admit. But I need someone like you, Coralie, you're kind and thoughtful, you'd sort of soften me up. I'm no fool and I know when someone goes out of their way to spare my feelings. You've done that several times, although I must say that at other times you haven't exactly minced your words. And I don't think you're after my money, either. Oh, yes, I'm a wealthy man in my own right, and I'll be even better off when I control the business.

"I know you fancy Scarlett, but he's fought shy of marriage for years, so it isn't likely he'll change now. If he does, he'll have the pick of Yorkshire falling over themselves to oblige. You should forget any ideas you're harbouring about him, Coralie."

154

He looked at her and put out a stubby hand. "What do you say? Shall we give it a whirl?"

She hesitated, wondering how to refuse without damaging his self-esteem too drastically. She had often suspected that the brash, confident manner concealed an inner uncertainty.

"I'm sorry, Roger. I can't marry you. I—I don't love you."

"Love!" he said contemptuously. "Don't give me all that stuff. You like me a little, don't you?"

"Yes. I like you quite a lot."

"Well then, let's take it from there."

"I'm sorry, Roger." There was a finality and a hint of regret in her voice.

He jumped to his feet. "It's Scarlett, isn't it?" he asked thickly.

Unable to see any point in denying it, she said, "Yes, it is. I can't help it, Roger. I didn't calmly sit back and say to myself 'Scarlett's quite a catch, I'll fall for him.' It just—happened. He doesn't even suspect how I feel about him, and I'm quite sure he looks on me just as a troublesome but rather valuable employee."

"I see." And perhaps he did, because the expression on his face at that moment held sympathy and a fleeting tenderness. He offered her his hand. "Come on, then. Let's get back before dark. I shall ask you again in a few weeks' time."

She was relieved that he'd taken it so well, and made no move to draw away when he put his arm lightly around her shoulders as they walked back to Raxhead.

"I'll be off then," he said, on their return, and without more ado opened the door of his car.

Relief and a touch of remorse made her lean forward to kiss him gently on his fair sunburnt cheek. "Goodnight, Roger."

He made no attempt to return the kiss, but just looked up at her from his seat behind the wheel. "Goodnight, Coralie," he said soberly, and drove off.

She felt restless and on edge when he had gone. The light was on in her bathroom, evidence that Francine was enjoying a leisurely bath, so on impulse she went round to the back of the house and climbed the stone staircase to the studio, thinking that half an hour on her black and white outline sketches for the catalogue would calm her down a little.

As always the room exerted its own tranquil spell upon her; the odour of raw wool and oil paints, the countless coloured skeins hanging from the rows of hooks on the wall, the absolute silence. Within minutes she was peacefully drawing at the board, with only one powerful lamp switched on, angled to shine on her work.

She bent over her drawing and the fanciful notion came to her that before coming to Raxby her life had been like an intricate tapestry made up of a variety of wools all blended together to form a harmonious but slightly monotonous whole. Then had come her interview at the Dorchester, and the brilliant colour that was Scarlett had exploded the peaceful subtle shades of her life, threading it with the vivid disturbing power of his personality.

When her eyes strayed to the twist of red wool in its little case by the door she realised where such an image had originated. Once that soft, faded wool had been brilliant; dyed by Scarlett's forbears, ambitious, clever men who had left their home county for a new life many miles away. . . .

When the door opened she was only a little surprised to see him standing there. He had been so alive in her thoughts that his appearance back at Raxhead seemed the logical outcome of her daydream.

She slid from the stool and walked towards him, leaving the circle of light under the lamp.

"Mr. Scarlett! You're back."

"I've been back quite some time," he replied coolly.

"But you were doubtless too busy with the boy-friend to notice."

It took several seconds for his words to register. "What? Oh! Yes—I went for a walk with Roger."

"Over the hills. In the dark." Cruelly he mimicked her tone. "And came back wrapped in his arms as usual."

"Why are you in such a rage?" she asked abruptly. "I went for a walk with Roger—a perfectly innocent stroll along the track. And yes, he had his arm round me as we walked back. What has that to do with you?"

"Nothing," he snapped. "Except that I'm getting a little tired of seeing Greenfield slobbering all over you in public, that's all!"

With an effort she controlled her anger and said with what she thought was great restraint, "As a matter of fact, he asked me to marry him."

At that a change came over Scarlett. Dark as it was by the door she saw him lose colour. The deep shadows cast by the lamp emphasised the bone structure of his face, which suddenly stood out bleached and skull-like, as if the flesh had fallen away.

"How strange," he said cynically, "I thought he already enjoyed all the privileges of matrimony without any of the responsibilities."

She stared at him, speechless, her mind whirling with suitably cutting replies, but her tongue refusing to form the words. And then at last, each word an icicle, she said slowly and distinctly: "I should have thought you would be the last one to talk about the responsibilities of marriage. At least Roger hasn't tried to persuade me to run off and live with him, and up to now, as you can see, I'm alive and well, not dead beneath the snow!"

At that his head jerked back hard, then the dark-lashed eyelids came down, covering the sockets in the skull-like face.

"Very clearly put," he said.

But Coralie wasn't finished. The built-up tension of the last few months was finding an outlet. She walked straight past him and ran back to the flat. She rushed into the bedroom and snatched the blood-stained evening dress and jacket from her wardrobe, then to Francine's astonishment she raced out again, hesitating for a moment this time as she wondered if he would still be in the studio or back in the house.

Breathless now, she ran up the stone steps and flung open the door. He was still there, exactly where she had left him, with something twisted in his hands.

She switched on the lights and stood in front of him, her hair in a wild disorderly swirl around her face. "If you examine this dress and jacket you'll see that they are stained with something. It's blood—Roger's blood. We saw an accident on the way home—*after* I had refused to spend the night with him, I might add—and he cut his hand badly. There was blood everywhere. He wasn't really fit to drive, and when I'd bandaged his wrist back here I knew he would have to stay the night. Hardly the privileges of matrimony, sleeping on the settee after losing a great deal of blood, and then being sent off home immediately after breakfast!"

She threw the dress and jacket on to the work-bench, and feeling the need for a final gesture, picked up her pile of sketches. Then she turned to leave, her point made.

It was then she saw what was in his hands. He held the skein of faded red wool, ripped apart, ruined. On the wall, just level with his throat, the glass front of the case was in fragments. A long jagged piece hung precariously by a remnant of some ancient adhesive. With a hollow tinkle it fell to the floor and shattered.

She looked into his face. Now that the lights were on she could see that his awful skull-like appearance must have been an illusion due to the deep shadows. What she saw now was the awful greyish pallor which she remembered from that night when she had been lost in the mist. The pallor, and a completely blank expression which concealed whatever was in his mind.

With a deep intake of breath she walked past him for the second time, her step as laboured as that of a very old woman, and went slowly back to the flat.

Ten

After a sleepless night it was difficult to present a cheerful front to Francine at breakfast, but Coralie was determined that her mother should go back home with an easy mind.

Soft summer rain was falling as they kissed goodbye on the platform, but only when the train was out of sight did Coralie give way to tears. In that moment of parting it seemed that her mother was taking away everything that was sane and normal, leaving her prey to all the sickening doubts and uncertainties of life in Raxby.

She walked back to the car, rain mingling with the tears on her cheeks, and then sat behind the wheel for a moment to compose herself.

The long hours of the night had brought the realisation that it would be impossible to follow the instincts which urged her to resign immediately. Whatever her personal relationship with Scarlett she simply couldn't abandon her work at this crucial stage. True, her actual designs were all completed, and any day now Greenfield's would start producing the full range, but there were still the final stages of the catalogue to work on.

She had promised Scarlett her help in deciding the layout and design of it, and was currently doing a series of outline sketches to complement the photographs.

But she was well aware that a condition of her employment had been a month's notice on either side. It was Friday—she could resign today and leave in four weeks if only she could finish what must be done before that time was up. The memory of what had passed between her and Scarlett decided her.

She dried her eyes and drove to work with a feeling of infinite relief at the prospect of getting away from the nerve-wracking torment of constantly being on bad terms with him.

It was when she entered the studio that the full realization of what she would be leaving hit her. Liz was sewing, and Coralie could hear her tuneful contralto as she sang over her work. The studio had never seemed so spacious and airy, so well-equipped, as it did at that moment. She looked out at the moors, wet beneath a troubled sky, knowing that she had grown to love their dramatic changes of mood, and the thought of leaving the wild lonely beauty of them filled her with despair.

Nevertheless, as soon as she had planned the day ahead with Liz she sat down and wrote a formal resignation, put it in an envelope and without further delay took it to Scarlett's office. She had no desire to see him if it could be avoided, so she asked Miss Silverwood to hand it to him as soon as possible.

The secretary smiled amiably. "He's not too busy just now, Coralie, if you want to see him in person. No? Oh well, I suppose you have a great deal to do in the studio. As a matter of fact I have a note here for you from Mr. Scarlett. I was going to pop along with it later."

She handed Coralie an envelope bearing Scarlett's unmistakable handwriting, and if she thought it strange that they had suddenly taken to communicating in writing she was too tactful to say so.

Coralie hurried back to the studio, handling the envelope in much the same way she would have held a loaded revolver.

The message was brief, without benefit of a salutation: "I feel there is little point in going ahead with our arrangement for dinner tomorrow evening. I am sure that to cancel it will be as much a relief to you as it is to me. J.J.S."

She stared at the forceful script and then read it through a second time. It was a brush-off both brutal and succinct! Any lingering hopes of a reconciliation disappeared once and for all before the cold, unemotional tone of the message.

Coralie lifted her chin. He had merely saved her the trouble of cancelling the date herself, that was all.

The phone rang. It was Roger, ostensibly with a query about one of the designs, but in reality to check that they were still on good terms after his proposal the previous evening. With an effort she kept her tone affable. After all, the man had done her the honour to propose marriage, and it cost nothing to be civil.

With a blinding headache and a dull pain beneath her breast-bone Coralie started work.

Five minutes later the phone rang again, and on hearing the familiar deep tones her heart gave a great, painful leap. "Could you spare a moment to come to my office, Coralie?"

She smiled grimly to herself. What would be his reaction if she said "No"?

"Yes, I'll be along directly, Mr. Scarlett."

Quickly she slipped out of her smock and smoothed her hair, which felt hot and sticky against her neck. The days of tying it back with an off-cut of cloth were long since gone, so she washed her hands in cold water and held a damp tissue against her forehead to cool herself, and then went along the corridor.

He was standing by the window when she arrived, but he quickly brought forward a chair for her, and placed it on the opposite side of the desk to his own. Then he sat facing her, eyeing her dispassionately.

She searched his face for some sign that he felt as terrible as she did, but the only visible marks of

162

stress were faint black shadows beneath the brilliant eyes. On his right hand was a large adhesive dressing. Quickly she shut her mind to the memory of the shattered glass of the little showcase.

"I've read your resignation, Coralie," he said quietly. "It is, I take it, a result of our confrontation last night?"

"In part, yes," she agreed briefly.

"I see. You had thought of resigning before last night, then? Apart from the day you arrived, that is?"

She stared at him unblinkingly, faint colour rising beneath her tan. "Yes. Occasionally."

"Because you weren't happy here?"

"Yes. But in any case, I reckon that in about four weeks' time my work on the scheme will be finished. If it's a success and you decide to go ahead with a spring and summer collection you'll have plenty of time to replace me."

"To replace you," he repeated slowly, pressing his lips together thoughtfully. "Have you mentioned to anyone that you have handed in your resignation."

"No, of course not. Not until I had told you."

"I see. Is it, perhaps, that you feel you deserve an increase in salary?"

"No, it's not!" she said indignantly. "If I thought I deserved a raise I would ask for one, not resign!"

"Quite." He paused, then said suddenly. "Now listen to me, Coralie. I'm asking you to withdraw this"—he flicked her letter of resignation with one lean brown finger. "It's foolish to let what went on between us at a personal level goad you into resigning. All right, I accept that there may be other reasons behind it as well, but I can do little about those if I don't know what they are.

"We both said things last night which I regard as unforgivable, but I'm not a man who finds it easy to reel off apologies nineteen to the dozen, so I suggest we both try to forget what was said. Nor, for that matter, am I a man who will plead; but I'm asking you now, in my capacity as Managing Director of this firm, to reconsider your resignation. Leave it in abeyance, if you like, just between you and me, and if you still feel the same when the catalogue is published you can leave at a moment's notice. What do you say to that?

"You have some holiday due to you, why not finish your part of the scheme to your satisfaction, and then take a long holiday before making a final decision?"

He waited for her answer, the vivid gaze oddly intent. His persuasive powers were quite something, she thought in confusion. But in fact his suggestion was both generous and sensible. She could see now that to resign from her marvellous job because of a personal quarrel would be foolish. Not only that, it would imbue their relationship with far more importance than Scarlett, for one, seemed to think it merited.

"All right," she said. "I agree to that arrangement."

He bent his head to examine her letter, rather as though he expected to find it suddenly re-written. "Good," he said briskly, "we'll leave it at that for now." Then he asked, "Did you know that we always hold a works party in August, just before the annual holiday? This year I'm hoping it will coincide with the news that the scheme is a success. After all your hard work I think you should be there, Coralie. Everyone goes, from the canteen ladies and the man who sweeps the yard, to the weavers and the board of directors. Helen comes as well—it's the one link she still retains with the firm."

"I'd like to go," agreed Coralie sedately.

He looked at her searchingly, then asked, "You got my note?"

"Yes, thank you."

"Any comment?"

"No—except that you saved me the trouble of writing a similar one to you."

Scarlett studied his finger-nails minutely. "I see. From now on, then, we'll keep strictly to business."

There were times during the next month when Coralie recalled his words with grim amusement. Life was so busy that there was little opportunity to do anything but keep strictly to business! The completing of her work on the catalogue was followed at once by the arrival of the models and Ben, the photographer, a lanky Australian with prematurely grey hair who had been engaged on Janice's recommendation. Marcelle, the older model, proved to be blessed with a great sense of humour, and when the stress of working to a deadline began to tell on them all, it was often her dry witticisms which relieved the tension.

The working committee had agreed to Coralie's suggestion of using the mill, Raxby village, and the surrounding countryside as backgrounds, and during the five hectic days of taking photographs she was constantly on hand to help with fittings and advise on the best views of her designs.

Not having seen Janice for several weeks she realised anew that the other girl was exceptionally sweet-natured. Coralie just couldn't help liking her. In addition to that, she soon saw that the clothes modelled by her always looked superb. She seemed to sense even more quickly than the other two just what Ben was aiming for, and her lovely piquant face and elegant figure showed off Coralie's designs beautifully.

During the time she was modelling, Scarlett apparently forgot his preference for a solitary snack at lunch-time. If shots were being taken in the country he would appear on the scene at mid-day and whisk Janice away for lunch, sometimes on her own, sometimes accompanied by Ben.

One day he joined the whole party at a table on the terrace over the river. Coralie was lunching with Roger that day, and at his request they were at a table

165

for two away from the others. Roger watched Scarlett for a moment without comment, then turned to Coralie and asked, "Do you still feel the same about him, or am I back in the running again?"

She sighed faintly. His continued assumption that her feelings for Scarlett were no more than a passing fancy, soon to be discarded in favour of a more permanent relationship with himself, was beginning to wear her down.

It was true that to some extent she had become resigned to the coldness between her and Jethro. At least she knew now where she stood with him, and accepted that there had never been more than interest and a certain respect for her on his part. She accepted also, without bitterness, that the concern which had been so apparent in his early dealings with her had declined abruptly as the mail-order scheme progressed. Hadn't she always known that it had been part of his "Keep Coralie happy" campaign?

Only in the silence of the night did she allow herself to dwell on that bitter scene in the studio up at Raxhead. It was during those lonely, sleepless hours that the sight of his lean, strong hands holding the ripped-apart skein of wool came back to torment her. He had treasured that soft, faded relic. Why then, had he destroyed it?

She rejected the logical answer to that, flatly refusing to let remorse for what she had said overcome her. He had been unforgivably outspoken and rude, and she had replied in a similar vein. He himself had suggested that they both forget what had been said, and—

"Coralie!" It was Roger, waiting for an answer.

"I'm sorry, Roger." She shook her head and tried to smile as they left the table. It was her stock reply and she was getting a little tired of repeating it.

And then suddenly, four weeks to the day after she tried to resign, the rush was over. The photographs were long since selected and the catalogue checked and printed. The studio was cleared and Liz, to her delight, was put in charge of the new mailing department.

Coralie cleared away her sketching materials, said goodbye to Liz, and left the mill for her month's holiday.

The completion of her mammoth task brought its own particular satisfaction, but she felt the urge to get away from Raxby, to walk the soft green hills of Somerset, to be with her mother and to see her friends.

Judith and Walter had been up to the flat for a sherry with her, and now the place was clean and sparkling, and Coralie was ready for the long drive home next day. Jethro had gone off somewhere in the two-seater, she had heard the familiar note of the engine whilst she was in the bath. On impulse she went across to the studio—the first time she had entered the room since that awful night.

It was silent in there, as always. Everything was tidy, and her sea-green dress was folded neatly away on a low shelf. She saw that the remains of the little show-case had been removed from the wall and the screw-holes filled in and painted over. It might never have existed.

She looked sadly at the many-coloured wools on their rows of hooks, remembering her strange flight of fancy about the thread of Scarlett brightening her life. What an emotional, imaginative fool she was!

Impatiently she brushed away the tears and ran down to the yard. The two-seater was back, parked at the front of the house, and Scarlett was helping Janice out of the passenger seat.

Quickly Coralie crossed the yard and climbed the stairs to her flat. The sooner she was away from Raxhead and its owner the better.

The time at home passed with incredible slowness, the only events of any real interest to Coralie being when she saw all the adverts for the Scarlett catalogue in the press, and when she opened a Sunday colour supplement and saw a superb two-page spread featuring her creations.

Francine was thrilled. "But your designs look marvellous!" she cried proudly, examining the pictures. "They are really beautiful, Coralie. Are you not pleased?"

"I shall be pleased if we receive orders for them," said Coralie drily. She found herself worrying constantly about whether any orders had been received. Only the fact that she had promised herself a complete break from affairs at the mill prevented her from ringing up and finding out how many catalogues had been sent out, and how many orders, if any, had resulted.

Day succeeded golden day, and her tan grew more spectacular. She helped Francine in the house and garden, and played tennis daily with her friends. But she found the break from work irksome rather than enjoyable, and had a hard time concealing her boredom from Francine.

It was with a feeling of relief that at last she went back to Raxby, travelling on a Thursday in order to be there in time for the works' dance the following evening. Any final decisions about resigning could be made in the light of the scheme's success or failure.

It was raining when she stopped at the phone box to tell Francine of her safe arrival, and as she drove up the lane to Raxhead the swish of the tyres on the wet road sounded sweetly in her ears. She ran up the steps to the flat eagerly. Jethro or no Jethro, it was good to be back.

She found a note from Judith, inviting her to have "a bite" in the kitchen, so after unpacking she went across to the house.

The housekeeper surveyed Coralie keenly and

greeted her in her usual undemonstrative manner. "You're back then," she said placidly. "Sit down and have something to eat, you look as though you could do with it."

Obediently Coralie sat at the big kitchen table and helped herself to cold chicken and ham. "Have you heard anything about how things are going at the mill, Judith? With the mail-order scheme, I mean."

She was infuriatingly vague. "I can't say I've heard much, really. Bella was here last night, but she didn't say anything. You'll have to ask Mr. Scarlett about it."

"Is he at home?" Coralie looked over her shoulder, half-expecting to meet that blank, impersonal stare.

"No," said Judith. "He's in the Lake District at Miss Helen's today. The children have had measles so he's been over there several times. If they're a bit better he'll bring her back tomorrow for the dance."

With that Coralie had to be content. She decided to go to the mill first thing next day to find out from Liz how things were going.

But next morning, to her surprise, Liz was non-committal about the orders received so far. She had greeted Coralie warmly, but on the subject of orders she was oddly unforthcoming. "Well—it's hard to tell. J.J. thinks these are early days and he says we mustn't worry. . . . Oh yes, we've had quite a few orders. No, no particular model is selling better than the others. . . ."

Coralie stared at her in perplexity. There was something oddly evasive about her friend's manner. If it had been anyone other than Liz, Coralie would have sworn she was concealing something, and not making a very good job of it, either.

All at once it dawned on her. Things were going badly and Liz didn't know how to tell her. That was it! Hurriedly she made some excuse and went down to the weaving shed, her thoughts in chaos. At least she wouldn't have to agonise about her resignation—if the scheme was a flop Scarlett would probably fire her.

She was amazed when she passed the works dining hall. It was being transformed with flowers, streamers and wall hangings. The terrace had been temporarily roofed over, and long buffet tables were being erected out there. People were swarming around, working at top speed. It seemed strange not to see Jethro's tall form striding through such a scene of activity, issuing orders, asking questions. Strange, and yet typical of the man, thought Coralie, to absent himself from preparations for the year's most important social function at the mill in order to visit two little girls with measles.

Quickly she left the hammering and sawing and drove off in the direction of Leeds, determined not to return to Raxby until the evening.

In a subdued frame of mind she dressed for the dance. It had seemed pointless to make something new when she had not yet worn the pink and gold dress made for her dinner date with Jethro. She had designed it to show off her best points—her narrow waist, her smooth golden shoulders and back, and she saw that it not only showed them off, but emphasised them and echoed her golden colouring in a way that made her almost beautiful.

Her hair, bleached and streaked by the sun, looked positively dazzling piled on top of her head in a top-knot, and her superb deep-gold skin shone with youth and health. She made up carefully, darkening her lashes and using her new bronze eye-shadow to highlight the enormous tawny eyes. Finally she slipped on the flimsy gold sandals which she had bought in Somerset, sprayed her shoulders with *Fleurs Fraiches* and surveyed the final effect in the mirror.

Considering that she felt terrible it was a surprise

to see that she looked radiant and full of vitality. The boring weeks at home must have done her some good, after all. And then, once ready, she realised that she had no idea of what time to arrive.

Slowly, as if in a slow-motion dream sequence, she put on the Sibelius symphony. Inevitably it brought to mind the night when she had invaded Scarlett's study and he took her hands in his, causing that deep, bell-like note to echo in her heart. That had been one of the very few times he had touched her. Oh, there had been that gentle "Keep Coralie happy" kiss, and the time he had carried her home from the moor, pressed so close to the warmth of his chest that she had almost felt his heart-beat. . . . And that was all, apart from one or two vice-like grips and maybe a few shoves and pushes. Not much to look back on in the years ahead. . . .

When the bell rang she thought it was Roger, although she was not expecting him to call for her. But it was Jethro who stood there, looking stunningly bronzed and handsome in a midnight blue dinner jacket. She held the door open wide, at once forgetting her resolve to be cool and distantly polite. "Mr. Scarlett! Come in. How are you?"

"I'm well, Coralie. And you? Have you had a good holiday?"

"Restful," she admitted with her customary honesty. "But a bit boring."

He laughed, but almost at once fell serious again as he looked at her. "That's a beautiful dress," he said slowly.

"Thank you. I made it for—I made it several weeks ago."

The brilliant eyes flickered, and she knew at once that he had guessed for what occasion it had been intended.

"I've come to see if you'll come down to the dance with Helen and me," he said. "She's looking forward to seeing you again."

"And I'm looking forward to it as well," said Coralie sincerely. "I'd love to come with you both. I'm ready now, I'll just switch off this record."

If the Sibelius brought back any memories for him he gave no sign, merely standing by the door with an expression of polite patience.

But Coralie had something on her mind, and no intention of waiting any longer to have her fears confirmed.

"Mr. Scarlett," she said urgently. "Is there any news yet about how it's going? I can't find out from anyone so far."

"Well," he replied, "nothing really definite has been confirmed yet by the fellows who claim to be able to forecast how it will go. Don't worry about it now, you've done all you can possibly do. We might know more in a day or two." And with that he turned to go.

With a little shrug Coralie picked up her handbag and followed him. Perhaps after all it was too early to know anything definite.

It was good to see Helen again and to be reassured that Alexandra and Emma were recovering speedily. Coralie felt grateful to Helen that she had been spared an unescorted arrival at the first social event she had attended at the mill.

A band was playing in the hall, and lights were strung above the terrace, spangling the busy waters of the river with colour.

Jethro had been quiet so far, leaving Helen and Coralie to chat together. Now he led them straight to the hall, and as the doors opened Coralie gained a lightning impression of an immense throng of people filling the long room to overflowing. She thought she saw Jethro raise his hand, and at once the band stopped playing and silence fell upon the room. Quite the dramatic entry, she thought, looking up at him curiously, and then there was applause and a wave of sound as people called out.

He left Helen by the door, and taking Coralie's arm

led her through the crowd. Still a little confused, Coralie blushed and tried to draw away. What on earth was he doing—dragging her so conspicuously to the platform? She caught sight of Liz's puggy little face wreathed in smiles, and then passed Janice, Zelda and Marcelle in the crowd; Ben too, and Miss Silverwood nodding and smiling.

The room became quiet again as Scarlett held up his hand. "Ladies and Gentlemen. As you all know, a talented team has been working for many months on the planning and shaping of a mail-order scheme for clothes made from Scarlett cloths. If a success, this scheme will ensure prosperity for Raxby and full production at the mill, something which in one way or another affects almost everyone present tonight.

"I have at my side Coralie Dee, designer of the clothes, and," he waved a sheet of paper, "I have in my hand confirmation that the scheme is off to a wonderful start, so good in fact that there is no doubt that it will be an outstanding success. The working committee are unanimous in stating that this success is due largely to the work and talent of Miss Coralie Dee. I ask you to join me, ladies and gentlemen, in showing our appreciation of her efforts."

With a flourish worthy of any master of ceremonies, Scarlett turned to Coralie and applauded. The room exploded in sound as everyone joined in, while Coralie, rendered quite speechless, turned first crimson and then shockingly pale beneath the golden tan.

He at once slid a supporting hand under her arm. "Are you all right, Coralie? It was all planned to be a pleasant surprise, not a shock."

She smiled shakily. "It's a surprise right enough. I'd already convinced myself that things were going badly." She looked helplessly at the packed hall. "I don't have to say anything, do I?"

"No," he said gently. "Just smile and say thanks

and then mingle with the crowd. I'll talk to you shortly."

And then a fair-haired boy whom Coralie recognised as being an apprentice dyer came forward and presented her with an enormous bouquet. She was touched, and, eyes bright, she looked up at Jethro. He was watching her with a look that was almost tender, and she felt her heart give that painful, traitorous leap.

The band started to play a waltz, and Roger came to her side at once, swinging her on to the dance floor before she could speak to anyone. Over his shoulder she saw Jethro cross the room and ask Mrs. Watson, a grey-haired weaver, to dance.

She was put-out at the way Roger had annexed her so quickly. She would have liked to find Liz to discuss the news of the scheme's success, and she had even, for a moment, thought that Jethro was about to ask her to dance.

Roger was subdued, due no doubt to the letters they had exchanged, and his phone calls while she was at home. She had made it clear, as gently as possible, that there was no future in their relationship except friendship. Outwardly he had accepted this, but his speed at partnering her proved that he still held hopes of staking his claim.

The waltz finished, and for Coralie the next hour was so filled with handshakes, congratulations, talk with Zelda and Marcelle, introductions between Helen and Liz, that afterwards she was quite unable to recall it in any detail. But all the time part of her mind was on Scarlett. How could she stay on at her job without driving herself mad with frustration at the gulf between them? Yet if it was true that she had played a vital part in the scheme's success how could she leave?

The last dance before supper was announced, and when Jethro claimed Janice as his partner Coralie left the room before Roger could find her. The sight of that dark elfin head against Scarlett's shoulder had plunged her into sudden irrational despair.

The lights were on in the stair-tower of the mill, and seeking solitude, Coralie lifted her skirts and climbed the wide stone steps which led to the tower roof. It was deserted up there—the only light came from the beam of the floodlights illuminating the Scarlett flag flapping quietly against its pole beneath a calm, starlit sky.

She knelt on a wooden bench and leaned over the parapet, looking down at the brightly-lit terrace and thinking of Jethro.

"Coralie!" He spoke her name quietly as if to avoid startling her, but even so she jumped to her feet in surprise at his silent approach.

"I saw you come up here," he said, his deep voice low, "and I wanted to talk to you alone. No one will disturb us, I've locked the tower door."

Amazed, she stared at him. "Locked the door? But I thought you were dancing with Janice?"

"Yes," he said carelessly, "so I was, but I handed her over to Ben."

Coralie thought his tone was reminiscent of someone stating the whereabouts of a troublesome kitten.

"First of all," said Jethro, handing her a slip of paper, "here is the bonus I promised you. I've doubled it, out of gratitude for your hard work and loyalty."

Two thousand pounds? She swallowed nervously, her throat dry. "But you mustn't, not yet. I mean—you can't—"

"I can," he said decisively. "Please take it and don't fuss."

She held the cheque hesitantly, her head reeling with the events of the evening and with the knowledge that she had the ideal opportunity now to tell him something—something that had been on her mind for many weeks past. She opened her lips to speak.

"Wait!" commanded Jethro, and to her astonishment he took her bag from her unresisting grasp, put the cheque inside it, and laid it on the bench. Then he took hold of her wrists, and lifting her arms so that they were outstretched towards him, he said calmly: "First move in the battle against Greenfield."

With that cryptic announcement he slid his hands slowly up her arms until he grasped the soft flesh above her elbows. Then deliberately and effortlessly he pulled her towards him, bent his dark head, and kissed her lips.

All the pent-up longing in Coralie's loving heart rose to meet the restrained passion of that kiss. His lips tasted clean and very fresh, and her confused thoughts and fears vanished beneath the sheer physical joy and excitement of being in his arms. She felt his hands, hard and very strong beneath her shoulder blades, pressing her closer, so that the softness of her breasts was crushed against his chest. With an unconsciously sensuous movement she stretched further on tiptoe, twined her arms tighter around his neck and kissed him back with enthusiasm.

And then the impact of what he had just said hit her, and she drew back, conscious that she had betrayed her feelings all too clearly. He released her at once, but kept hold of her wrists, looking down at her with a rather stunned expression.

"What do you mean—the battle against Greenfield?" she asked breathlessly.

"I mean that I'm not going to let him have you without a fight," he answered. "Though Heaven only knows I can't blame him for wanting you if you kiss him like you've just kissed me!"

She gaped at him. "What did you say?"

Obligingly, he repeated it.

Coralie thrust out her lips mutinously. "If you could bring yourself to believe what I say for once, I'd like you to know that the only time I have kissed Roger willingly was the night you saw us, after he'd proposed to me, and then it was a mere peck on his cheek."

"Is that so?" he said disbelievingly. "Not very encouraging for a prospective husband, I must say."

She stared at him, her great golden eyes puzzled. "But I refused him! And what's more I've refused him several times since."

For the first time since they met she saw him at a loss.

"But—I've been expecting you both to name the day." He glared at her angrily. "You never told me you'd refused him!"

"You never asked me," she pointed out reasonably. "It isn't my fault that Roger likes me. I've not given him the slightest encouragement, but he won't leave me alone. Whereas—" Abruptly she fell silent.

He released her wrists and finished off the sentence for her. "Whereas I showed no interest in you?"

She shook her head. "You were more than kind," she protested, "but I thought it was just because you wanted me kept happy so that I would 'deliver the goods' with my designs."

At that he groaned out loud. "Coralie, get this into your beautiful head once and for all. I have loved you since the moment I first set eyes on you at the Dorchester, when you walked into my life like the essence of spring itself. From the beginning I longed to shower you with clothes and jewels and every luxury I could think of, but you were so independent, so determined to be the employee and keep me firmly in my place as your employer." His eyelids fell, veiling the brilliant eyes for a moment. "You couldn't even bring yourself to call me by my first name, but with Greenfield it was 'Roger' from the word go."

She looked up at him, remorse stabbing her. How different it all sounded when told from his point of

177

view. "I'm sorry," she said gently, "truly sorry for any unhappiness I've caused you. But you *were* a bit intimidating, you know, and I was terrified that you'd guess how I felt about you."

"Felt about me?" he repeated slowly.

"I've never kissed any man as I just kissed you," she said simply. "I love you, Jethro Scarlett."

At that he took her in his arms again, his lips against her shining hair.

"But I never thought—although to be honest I was a bit puzzled at times. I thought you loved Roger, and yet sometimes you seemed to—to look at me in a certain way. And then after the plane crash Judith told me on the phone that you were very upset. That raised my hopes, and like a love-sick boy I came dashing home to see for myself just how upset you were. Then you greeted me so coolly and politely, I felt a conceited fool for having imagined you might care for me."

"But you see," said Coralie earnestly, "I thought you and Janice were—were lovers."

The statement hung on the air between them. "*Janice*? But she's always been like a sister to me. A sort of zany career-girl sister who needed someone to keep an eye on her. I'm very fond of her, just as I am of Helen. And in any case, I thought you knew that she is seriously interested in Ben."

It seemed as if a heavy load was being lifted, piece by piece, from Coralie's heart. He led her to the bench, and sat facing her, holding her hands, as he continued. "I postponed telling you my feelings for one reason, over and above Roger and all our other mixups." He paused, remaining quite still and with his vivid eyes fixed intently on hers.

"Yes?" she prompted.

"I wanted to give you time to prove yourself at the job. You're only twenty-one, you've trained for three years in preparation for this chance, and I know you are good. I didn't want anyone to be able to say that you had succeeded due to my influence. I was so determined on that course that I let Roger snatch you from right under my nose. Do you wonder I was half mad with jealousy?"

"But—I still can't believe that you were," she said uncertainly.

At that he took hold of her bodily, lifting her across his knees and cradling her in his arms while he murmured foolish little baby-names over her. If anything could have convinced her of the reality of what was happening it was hearing those broken endearments from the self-contained Scarlett. She turned her face into the warmth of his throat, pressing her lips against the pulse which was beating there.

She had one more thing to straighten out with him. "Jethro," she began determinedly, and as she spoke his name he smiled his devastating smile, and silenced her with a kiss. After that it was a long time before she could bring herself to pull away from him to say her piece.

"For ages I've wanted to tell you how desperately sorry I am for what I said about Melanie's death on the moors. No wonder you were so furious that you—you ripped your skein of red wool to pieces." Her voice trembled at the recollection of his drawn skull-like face as he gripped the fragments of wool. "I—I know you treasured it."

He pressed gentle fingers under her chin and tipped her face up to his, slowly shaking his head. "It wasn't because of what you said about Melanie, although that stung, I admit. I smashed the glass and ripped the wool to pieces out of fury. Yes, fury with myself for letting Greenfield have you. I felt a crazy urge to punish myself for losing you, and as it happened my precious skein of wool was close at hand."

She was silent for a moment, the great amber eyes searching his face: "But you were right when you said afterwards that what we'd both said was unforgivable. I want you to know that I don't really

179

believe what I was told—that it was because of you she died. It doesn't fit your character. I don't believe it was your fault at all!"

He stayed quite motionless, his hands still cupping her chin. She wriggled uneasily at his lack of response, and the cool night breeze whispered around her bare shoulders. Immediately he stroked the silky skin with his firm, warm hands.

At last he spoke. "Thank you, Coralie, for your faith in me. But what I really referred to as unforgivable was what I said about Roger enjoying the privileges of matrimony. I was almost murderous at first when I knew he had stayed the night, but how could I protest? I had promised you more than once that you would be entirely free and unsupervised in the flat, and so I kept silent and tried very hard to make myself fall out of love with you. And my only excuse for that scene in the studio is that I had rushed round Copenhagen like a maniac in order to get back to you a day early, and the first sight to greet me was you and Roger coming home in each other's arms."

She sighed in understanding. "But—about Melanie?"

"You are right, as it happens, about it not being my fault. When I told you I had loved her, it was true. I did love her very dearly, although she didn't even like me—she was infatuated with my young brother, Ralph. I wasn't yet twenty-one, and still at university, but Ralph was only eighteen, and just up at Oxford."

Scarlett paused, as if the memories were still fresh and painful. "It was Ralph who arranged to meet her. Ralph who persuaded her to run off with him. But at the last moment he panicked and went back early to Oxford, leaving me to sort things out at this end. He hadn't expected the blizzard, of course. Her parents were mad with grief at her death, and when they took it for granted that I was the man involved, I found it impossible to tell them that she had died for a boy of eighteen who already had a bad reputation with the girls. That's why people still link her name with mine, of course."

Coralie leaned back and looked at him, tears of sympathy and pride in her eyes.

He looked at her tenderly. "Don't cry for me, my darling. As I told you once before, those lovely golden eyes were made for laughter, not for tears. I swear that you'll never cry again because of me. If your mother will come to live in Raxby I'll buy her a house not far from Raxhead, if you think she'd like that. But don't let it be too long before our wedding, Coralie. How soon can it be?"

"Next week?" she suggested demurely.

With a delighted laugh he set her back on her feet. "I can see you're determined to make me wait," he said.

Together they looked out over the parapet to the hillside opposite, where the pale stone walls of Raxhead were just visible, backed by the great curving mass of the moors.

A burst of laughter came from below, and Scarlett glanced down at the brightly-lit scene. "Let's go and tell Helen and the others," he said. "I want everyone to know you're going to marry me."

With another kiss on her smiling lips he led her to the stairs. High above the tower the timeless stars shone, serene and still, but the great flag streamed out before a sudden breeze, and as Coralie turned for a last look she saw the thread of scarlet upon it leap and dance, as if in triumph. It had come into her life to stay.

ABOUT THE AUTHOR

RACHEL MURRAY is happily married and has three sons. The family lives in Gloustershire—Cotswolds country—but retains strong links with Rachel's native Lancastershire.

She started writing seven years ago and likes to experiment with various types of fiction, using pseudonymns.

Rachel is a keen cook; likes sewing, the movies, interior decorating—and travelling abroad.

In fact, the whole family plans a touring holiday in the United States in the summer of 1982.

CIRCLE OF LOVE

Step out of your world and enter the Circle of Love.

Six new CIRCLE OF LOVE romances are available every month. Here's a preview of the six newest titles on sale May 15, 1982:

#16 INNOCENT DECEPTION by Anne Neville (#21516-7 • $1.75)

It was a chance for Laurel to taste a life of unaccustomed luxury. But little did she realize the consequences of impersonating her glamorous, coldhearted twin sister—or how her own heart would betray her once she was thrust into the arms of Derek Clayton, her sister's estranged but wealthy husband.

#17 PAMELA by Mary Mackie (#21505-1 • $1.75)

Pamela woke in a hospital room with no memory of her past, no knowledge of her name. Her only thought was of her instant attraction to the hostile and handsome man before her. Pamela did not recall anything he told her of her past... and even worse, she felt herself plunging headlong into careless desire for this dangerously seductive man.

#18 SAND CASTLES by Alexandra Kirk (#21529-9 • $1.75)

Jason Kent always got what he wanted. And now he wanted Melissa to give up her independence and become governess to his young, motherless daughter. But could she cope with the desires which welled up in her heart when Jason was near? And could she stand to be so close to him—and watch him marry another woman?

CIRCLE OF LOVE

O

With Circle of Love Romances, you treat
yourself to a romantic holiday—anytime,
anywhere. Enter The Circle of Love—and
travel to faraway places with romantic
heroes. . . .

21502	GOLD IN HER HAIR	$1.75
21507	ROYAL WEDDING	$1.75
21500	DESIGN FOR ENCHANTMENT	$1.75
21510	THE HEATHER IS WINDBLOWN	$1.75
21508	GATES OF THE SUN	$1.75
21509	A RING AT THE READY	$1.75
21506	ASHTON'S FOLLY	$1.75
21504	THE RELUCTANT DAWN	$1.75
21503	THE CINDERELLA SEASON	$1.75